SWEET VICTORY

Beverly Lane

A KISMET® Romance

METEOR PUBLISHING CORPORATION
Bensalem, Pennsylvania

To Wilson and Kimball
. . . and to Evelyn

BEVERLY LANE

A former English teacher and businesswoman, Beverly is now a full-time writer and compulsive reader with a library of over three thousand books and an often-used library card. She lives in La Mesa, California, with her husband and their pets—a Rhodesian Ridgeback and a Lhasa Apso (a physically mismatched pair who adore each other), and a cat.

ONE

"Easy, Copper King," Kit Randall said, even though she knew the restless colt couldn't hear her over the noise of the crowd that separated them. "Easy," she repeated, but this time she spoke to herself, trying to hold back the tears that threatened to spill down her cheeks.

Beyond the red-tile-roofed barns and green paddocks of Randall Farm, golden-brown foothills shimmered in the heat of mid-July. That view, or the memory of it, had always comforted her. Today it didn't. Her tears welled again, stinging and hot, but she blinked them away.

The squeal of the microphone jerked her gaze back to the auctioneer pacing a stage placed in the shade of an oak tree. The wiry little man gestured with his hand-held microphone and jabbed a bony forefinger toward the colt in the rope-enclosed ring beside him.

"Nine hundred thousand is bid." He paused dramatically. *"Nine hundred thousand."*

An excited buzz greeted the announcement, but the little man set his lips and hunched his narrow shoulders. *Not good enough*, his posture told the crowd. "Ladies and gentlemen," he said, allowing a pleading note to creep into his voice, "remember that this colt is the son of the great Coppertown, the grandson of the immortal Black Moon Rising and"— he thrust out his thin arms like a tent revivalist— "he's from the last breeding planned by Oliver Randall, one of the greatest horsemen in the history of thoroughbred racing."

The auctioneer's voice rose and cracked on the last word. The colt, startled by the sound, increased the speed of his restless dance, his muscles rippling and bunching under his gleaming chestnut skin. Allowing himself a faint smile at the crowd's murmur of admiration, the auctioneer stepped to the edge of the platform and searched their faces. He rested his gaze on a striking redhead three rows ahead of Kit's last-row seat and raised his eyebrows in question.

The woman nodded.

"Nine hundred and fifty thousand is bid. Do I hear one million?"

A stunned silence followed the announcement, then a babble of voices. Marcella Wentworth's bid was the highest ever offered for a thoroughbred at a private California auction and the crowd knew it.

Kit smoothed wisps of damp blond hair from her sweaty cheeks, pasted a broad smile on her face, and prayed no one would notice the gleam of her tears.

Pretending that she wanted to sell the one horse she'd hoped to salvage from the ruin of Randall Farm demanded all her acting skill.

Jake Blaylock, her seventy-year-old farm manager, moved restlessly in the chair beside her, and she reached for his hand with both of hers. "Did you hear that? Copper King's going to bring a record price."

Jake's hand remained limp. "I heard it," he said glumly, "and I sure hope somebody bids a million. Oliver would twist in his grave if he thought Marci Wentworth and that brother of hers stood a chance of getting our colt."

"I don't like it any better than Daddy would have, but Marcella just made a record bid. Nobody's likely to top it."

The auctioneer cupped a hand to his ear. "Do I hear one million?"

When silence greeted the question, Jake slumped in his chair. "You're right. Marci's got him."

The little man stepped behind his lectern and lifted his gavel. "Going once at nine hundred fifty thousand, twice at nine hundred fifty—".

"One million."

The rich baritone voice came from behind Kit and she and the rest of the crowd turned toward it. A stranger leaned against the trunk of an oak, his massive shoulders hunched to accommodate its curve. Dappled sunlight cast a pattern of light and shadow over him, illuminating the coppery, angular planes of his face. Sweat glistened in his unruly black hair, plastered his white dress shirt to his chest like a breastplate, and gleamed in the hollow of his neck revealed by his open collar.

Seemingly oblivious to everything but the colt, he thrust his hands into the pockets of his gray slacks and rested the sole of his loafer against the tree trunk, revealing the curve of his buttocks and the massive strength of his thighs. The sound of feminine approval rippled through the crowd, but the stranger didn't seem to notice it.

Kit's gaze flickered over his still face. He wasn't handsome. His nose was slightly bent, his jaw too strong, but he was completely and compellingly masculine, exuding an electric vitality that crackled beneath his calm exterior.

In spite of the heat, a shiver shot up her spine and she dragged her gaze away, disgusted with herself. His looks and sex appeal didn't matter. What counted was his kindness and his compassion for the colt. *If* he outbid Marcella, who usually got what she wanted.

The auctioneer, seeming almost pleased by the amount of the bid, looked back at Marcella. "One million is bid. Do I hear a million fifty thousand?"

Marcella hesitated, then shook her head.

He lifted his gavel again. "Going once at a million . . ."

The stranger didn't move. He just smiled at Copper King until the auctioneer pounded his gavel.

Kit beckoned to Miguel, her head groom, who waited at the edge of the crowd to take Copper King back to the barn. "Please take Jake home. You can come back for Copper King. I think everyone would like a closer look at him now." *Everyone except Marcella*, she thought as she watched the woman stride toward a waiting limousine.

"But I want to meet the man who bought our colt," Jake protested.

"You can meet him later," she said, dropping her arm across his thin shoulders. "Now you need rest and some liquid. Please go with Miguel."

Jake put his hand on Miguel's forearm and turned reluctantly away, stumbling a little.

Sighing, Kit shook her head. Jake wasn't getting well as fast as she'd hoped he would, and if she lost him, too . . . She willed away the thought and began to thread her way through the crowd, stopping often to accept congratulations. She wondered what the enthusiastic well-wishers would think if they knew she was a fraud and a failure—that she had spent the two years since her father's death trying to keep the farm and the horses they were congratulating her for selling?

She was several yards from Copper King when he spotted her and lunged toward her, dragging the auctioneer's assistant behind him. "Whoa, boy," Kit said. "Not so fast. I didn't bring any carrots."

She ducked under the rope enclosing the ring and walked toward the horse, her movements hampered by her high-heeled sandals, which sank into the soft grass. "I'm sorry about that," she said to the handler, taking Copper King's lead rope. "He's quite a handful, but I think he'll settle down for me."

"Does he like you even when you don't bring carrots?"

She located the colt's new owner easily. At a couple of inches over six feet, he was taller than anyone in the small, mostly female group hovering around him. One of Kit's middle-aged neighbors simpered up at him and Kit felt embarrassed for her, but the man's clear gray gaze was on Kit. His smile was brilliant, white.

For the first time that day, Kit didn't have to force an answering smile. "He likes me. I seem to be able to calm him when no one else can."

"You're Kit Randall," he said, ducking under the rope to extend his hand.

"Yes." His gray eyes were striking, almost hypnotic in his dark face, with lashes so long and dark they looked painted on. "It's actually Katherine Randall. When I was six, I asked my family to call me Kit and the name stuck." The contact of his flesh with hers stunned her. She pulled her hand away, trying to force words from a mouth suddenly gone dry. "I . . . took the name from Kit Kat, one of the best mares we ever owned. It sounds silly now."

"I don't think it's silly. I'm Alejandro Menendez. Call me Alex."

"Congratulations on buying Copper King, Alex. I hope he wins lots of races for you."

Alex laughed. "I have a million reasons to want that, too."

Kit liked his laugh. It was uninhibited, and deep and rich like his voice. A strange little flutter began low in her belly. She tensed her muscles, but the feeling persisted. Damn! Her life had spun out of control and now even her hormones were on a rampage.

She tried to look away, but his gray gaze caught hers, held. As if the sound came from a great distance, she heard the colt moving again and vaguely felt his velvety nose run across her shoulders and down her arm.

"What's he doing?"

Her mind had slowed; her lips moved automatically. "Looking for . . . for those carrots. It's about time for his afternoon snack."

Copper King dropped his nose to the base of her spine and nudged her gently. Kit reached behind her to push him away. "Stop that! You'll have your carrots soon enough. It won't hurt you to meet your new owner."

The colt only nudged Kit again, harder this time, and she teetered precariously. "I guess I'd better have him taken back to the barn. He's—"

A third nudge thrust her forward—straight into Alex's arms! One shoe came off, everything in her purse spilled onto the grass, and suddenly, dizzingly, she became aware of the hardness of his body, his heat and dampness striking through her thin cotton sundress. Warmth spread up her cheeks. "I'm sorry . . ."

Alex held her waist, and when she tried to push herself away, he tightened his grip and smiled down at her. "It seems that Copper King has brought us together in more ways than one."

Not trusting her voice, Kit nodded. Her lashes fluttered down, but she knew he was still looking at her, and that others were watching, too. She felt her blush grow hotter.

Alex crouched and picked up her shoe. "Steady yourself on my shoulder," he said matter-of-factly, as if hungry colts pushed strange women into his arms every day.

All too aware of the onlookers, Kit rested her hand on his shoulder, careful not to lean any harder than necessary to maintain her balance. She raised her chin, stiffened her spine, and tried to salvage what was left of her dignity.

Copper King chose that moment to thrust his head under her arm and nuzzle Alex's hair. Laughter rippled through the crowd.

Seemingly unembarrassed, Alex smiled up at her. "His search for carrots never ends, does it?"

She pushed away the colt and slipped into her shoe. "Apparently not," she said stiffly, telling herself she'd only imagined that Alex had caressed the arch of her foot and that his fingers had lingered too long on her ankle.

They retrieved the scattered contents of her purse and stood at the same time. Alex's gaze probed hers, and she tried for an impersonal smile of thanks, but she knew she hadn't managed it well—that she probably looked like a schoolgirl smiling at the object of her first crush.

Kit looked vulnerable and soft and Alex wanted to kiss her. In fact, he might have kissed her if twenty or thirty people hadn't been watching. He suppressed a grin. Maybe he'd kiss her anyway. He'd love to see the shocked looks on those bland Anglo-Saxon faces if a guy named Alejandro Menendez kissed one of their princesses.

Thrusting his hands into his pockets, he resisted the temptation, contenting himself with looking at her. He'd have recognized Oliver Randall's daughter anywhere. She had her father's fine-boned, aristocratic look, his golden hair, deep-blue eyes, and proud carriage. But Oliver had been a tall man, and even in those ridiculous high-heeled sandals, Kit reached only to Alex's chin. With them off, she was probably about five three, and for the life of him, he couldn't imagine a more appealing sixty-three inches.

Her wrinkled and damp yellow sundress clung to her voluptuous curves in ways she probably hadn't intended when she put it on, and tendrils of hair that had escaped the loose knot atop her head clung wetly to her flushed cheeks. Her lipstick was almost gone, and what was left was slightly smudged. She looked as if she had just been made love to. His pulse kicked into high gear and he expelled a raspy breath. What was wrong with him anyway? He was here on business, not to fantasize about a lazy rich girl who'd ruined one of the best thoroughbred farms in the country.

He frowned across the unkempt lawn toward the broken tiles on one of the barns and remembered the first time he'd seen this place, with its immaculately tended grass and ponds and banks of flowers. And the horses! He'd never imagined that horses were born loving to run. He'd stood beside the paddocks for hours, watching even the tiniest foals race across the grass beside their mothers like autumn leaves before the wind.

Copper King threw up his head, jerking on the lead rope to signal his impatience. At least the colt was healthy. According to his buyer, all the horses had been in top-notch condition. Alex supposed that not even Kit Randall was careless or lazy enough to neglect the horses. They were money in the bank. Besides, she seemed to like Copper King.

She turned slightly, and Alex's gaze rested on her breasts. They were surprisingly full for such a small, slim woman, and the perspiration that sheened her body must be gathered in the deep valley between them. Her sweat would taste salty and smell sweet, and her skin would be . . . He cut off the thought, but she must have read something of what he was thinking because a fresh wave of color washed her cheeks. Her gaze skittered away from him and came to rest on a spot over his left shoulder.

He'd made her nervous and that meant she was aware of him as a man. He liked that. She probably wasn't used to the direct approach. The guys in her set—the silver-spoon crowd—had more leisure time to play games, but he'd always been a man in a hurry. He'd had to be.

A muscle in Alex's jaw tightened. *In a hurry for what?* To have a roll in the hay with a woman who'd destroyed the farm her father had devoted his life to? Alex's gaze narrowed on her face. "I think you should get my colt back to the barn," he said harshly.

*   *   *

Alex's words and his tone hit Kit with the force of a blow. "*My* colt," he'd said. Reflexively, she tightened her hand on Copper King's lead line, but as tightly as she tried to hold him, she had to accept that he wasn't hers anymore. She felt the all-too-familiar clutch in her throat, but she refused to let tears well into her eyes. She raised her chin a couple of notches. No one had ever seen a Randall cry and no one ever would.

Kit gazed up into Alex's angry face. The animosity coming from him was almost palpable. But why? What had she done? She stiffened, resisting his anger, resisting *him*. He'd bought her horse, that was all. What he thought of her, or she of him, didn't matter.

Catching sight of Miguel walking toward them, she gestured for him to hurry. "When will your men pick up Copper King?" she asked as coolly as she could manage.

A strange expression crossed his hard face. "We'll talk about that later," he said, glancing at his watch. "Right now, I'm late for an appointment. How about my stopping by tomorrow morning?"

"Fine." Kit extended her hand.

For an instant he touched it. "I warn you, I get up early."

Warmth began in her palm and flashed up her arm. "So . . . do I."

Later, when she could think, she decided Alex was surprised by her answer, but she couldn't be sure. He'd walked away too quickly.

* * *

For the dozenth time that morning, Kit threaded her way through the maze of cardboard cartons that littered the floor of her huge old kitchen. Somewhere in the mess was the roll of masking tape she needed to seal another box. She raked back her hair and swore softly. Moving was awful, and moving fifty years' worth of accumulated household items seemed almost impossible.

She'd just spotted the tape where it had rolled under the round oak table in the middle of the room when someone knocked on the kitchen door. The old-fashioned wall clock showed five-thirty. Too early for Jake, unless . . . Every muscle in her body snapped to attention and she strode to the door and jerked it open.

Alex stood on her doorstep, his eyes still heavy with sleep. "I was going to knock at the front door when I saw light coming from the back. I hope I didn't startle you."

Resisting the temptation to smooth back her hair, Kit forced a polite smile. When Alex had told her he got up early, she hadn't thought it would be *this* early. He'd caught her completely off guard, and she was a mess, a total disaster.

She'd French-braided her hair too hastily, and much of it had pulled loose to hang about her face; her jeans were so old they'd faded to white and were far too tight; she'd knotted her blue-and-gold Randall Farm T-shirt at the waist and it clung to her curves, clearly revealing she was braless.

Alex's gaze skimmed over her, lingered on her breasts, and came to rest on her face, devoid of makeup. Summoning all her poise, Kit gestured him inside. "When you knocked, I thought something had happened to Jake Blaylock, my trainer and farm manager. He had a heart attack several weeks ago, and he hasn't recovered as fast as I'd hoped he would."

Alex tripped on a tile, caught himself, and stepped into the room.

"I should have warned you that several of those tiles are broken."

"So I see."

His tone was so sharp that her gaze flew to his. She began to apologize for the tiles, but she stopped herself. Alex had come to make arrangements for Copper King. The farm was none of his business. She had already discussed the farm's condition with the agent for Summit Enterprises, the purchaser. The agent, speaking for the owner of the company, had agreed to buy the place in "as is" condition. If the purchaser could accept the place as it was, she'd be damned if she'd worry about Alex's reaction to it.

She cleared newspaper off a chair. "Won't you sit down?" she asked, her momentary irritation giving way to nervousness again. Somehow the large room didn't seem so big with Alex in it. It wasn't so much his height; she'd known taller men. It was the sheer size of him, the shoulders bulking so large beneath his blue oxford shirt, the powerful arms revealed by his rolled-back sleeves, the massive thighs straining against the seams of his jeans. The chair squeaked a protest when he sat down. She felt the sheer force of his intense gaze and her edginess increased.

"Would you like some coffee?" she asked in a voice she fervently hoped was calm.

"Sounds good." Alex glanced around the kitchen. "If I'd known you were so busy, I'd have come at a more convenient time."

"There's no convenient time. I've sold the farm and I have to be out on the last day of the month. Before then I have to pack the accumulated belongings of five lives—my parents', my grandparents', and my own. It's quite a job. Randalls have lived in this house for over fifty years."

"It must bother you to leave it."

Bother her? Leaving Randall Farm *devastated* her. It was her birthright, her identity, her link with the past. Leaving it would cause pain that would never go away. She turned the tap on full, hoping the sound of the water would drown out the huskiness in her voice. "Of course it bothers me, but it's time to move on and try something else. It's too easy to get stuck in a rut."

"It's the kind of rut a lot of people would love to get stuck in," Alex said sharply.

Startled by his vehemence, Kit drew in a long, shuddering breath before she answered. "People want different things from life. I'm as entitled to want to sell Randall Farm as others are to want to own it."

"Are you?" His voice cracked like a whiplash.

Kit's eyes rounded with shock that rapidly gave way to anger. He had no right to judge her, she thought furiously. Her gaze narrowed on the lean, hard lines of his face, then met his startling gray eyes without blinking. "Yes, I am," she said through gritted teeth.

His jaw clenched as if he were biting back words. Then he shrugged, but Kit knew he wasn't convinced. He simply didn't care enough about what she did with the farm to argue with her. She felt a prick of disappointment. Part of her spoiled for a fight. She needed an outlet for the anger and frustration that had built over the past two years. She'd like to kick holes in the boxes that littered the kitchen, throw plates, tear her hair, and scream at the top of her lungs.

Instead, she poured water into the top of the drip-coffee unit, placed the pot on the heating plate, and punched the "On" button. "How do you like your coffee?" she asked in a flat voice, taking two mugs from the cupboard.

"Black."

Kit nodded. She'd given up cream and sugar long ago. Strong black coffee sustained her better through the long nights she'd spent trying to track down the extent of her father's debts and agonizing over where she'd get the money to feed the horses and make the payroll.

"Have you found a new place?" Alex asked after she'd poured their coffee and sat down opposite him.

"No. I thought maybe I'd go back to Europe for a while."

"You've spent a lot of time in Europe." It was a statement, and she stared at him for a moment, surprised.

"I went to college at the Sorbonne. After I graduated, I . . . wandered . . . in Europe for another four years. I came back here two years ago just before my father died.''

''The life of a jetsetter must be taxing.''

Kit froze, then took a shaking breath. Did he really think she was a lazy, spoiled member of the international jet set who spent her time attending parties and suntanning on the Riviera?

She stared down at her calloused hands with their broken nails. They weren't the hands of a jetsetter, but if Alex noticed them, he probably thought she was too lazy to get a manicure. She bit her lower lip painfully, resisting her need to defend herself.

''You're right, jetsetting *does* take a lot of work.'' She let a note of sarcasm creep into her voice. ''Lying on the beach hour after hour is so boring I get a headache just thinking about it.'' She melodramatically pressed the back of her hand to her forehead. ''And those parties! Night after night, nothing but parties!''

A faint red flush crept along Alex's jawline and she let herself smile just enough to increase his irritation. She'd bet he wasn't used to being teased. At the thought, her grin widened.

His gray gaze slammed into hers and her smile slowly faded, her surroundings receded, her body stilled. Long moments passed. Then Alex smiled faintly in imitation of her smile and reality returned. He was playing a game with her!

Heat rose in her face and she stood so suddenly she had to grab the chair to keep it from toppling. He'd taken her harmless teasing to a personal level, exerting his mastery over her, showing her he recognized her attraction to him. Damn the man! She wished he'd choke on his coffee.

Summoning as much poise as she could muster, she said, "I need to get back to work." She carried her coffee to the sink and poured it out.

The door opened and Jake entered, leaning heavily on a cane she hadn't seen him use before. When he saw Alex, his tired face lit with a smile. "I wondered when I was going to meet the man who bought our colt," he said. He let Alex pull out a chair and settle him into it, nodding gratefully. Kit's lips tightened. Only a few days ago, he would have refused the help.

Alex's grin was almost boyish. "I've looked forward to meeting you, Mr. Blaylock. You're a legend in racing."

"Jake." The old man looked pleased, but he waved his hand dismissively. "I've been lucky to have great horses to train, and nobody could have asked for better bosses than the Randalls. Me and my wife Evvie—she passed away five years ago—we came from Indiana to work for Oliver Randall and his daddy in the fifties, and we never regretted it." He shook his head emphatically. "No, sir, not for a minute."

While Kit prepared Jake's breakfast, his voice droned in the background of her thoughts. Like everyone else, Jake had adored her father and admired his brilliance and his ability as a horseman. But Oliver Randall had never been interested in the bottom line. Money bored him, and he'd left that aspect of the farm's operations to his wife. After her death, he'd assured Kit he needed no help in running the place, and she'd believed him because she'd wanted to. She shook her head. What a fool she'd been! She'd never imagined her father would fail her.

Her sudden anger gave way to sadness. He'd failed himself, too, and in those last terrible months of his life thoughts of all he'd thrown away had haunted him. She'd seen it in his eyes and read it in the weary slump of his once-proud body. She cleared her throat and Jake and Alex looked curiously at her.

She set down Jake's breakfast of oat bran cereal, wheat toast, and orange juice and waited for his usual complaint about doctors who made him eat "women and kids' food." He only nodded his thanks, an ear-to-ear grin on his craggy face. Alex had charmed him and he'd talk for hours.

Kit was grateful that Jake's reminiscences put off the time when Alex would tell her about his plans to move Copper King. She'd tried to accept the loss of the colt, but the thought of never seeing him again left an empty place in her heart that would never be filled.

She wrapped a willow-patterned plate that had been precious to her grandmother and remembered the night she and her father had delivered the colt. They'd looked at each other over the tiny, still-wet creature struggling to stand and her father had said, "This is the one we've been waiting for, Kit." She'd nodded and they'd laughed and hugged each other. Three days later, her father died.

Not even Jake could fully understand what Copper

King meant to her. The colt was the best product of the Randalls' careful breeding program, the living link to all the generations of Randalls, and her father's triumph. The grooms had accused her of treating Copper King more like a Great Dane than a horse, and she supposed they were right.

Jake's voice surfaced again. "Yep," he said, slapping the table for emphasis, "the Wentworths and the Randalls were always rivals in the horse business. Marci and her brother Blane sure would have crowed if they'd gotten their hands on our colt. He's going to be the best, and they know it. We're real glad you got him."

Alex looked at Kit over the rim of his coffee cup. "Are you?"

Jake nodded. "Sure we are. Kit agrees with me about the Wentworths, especially Blane. She went out with him a few times while they were in high school." The old man winked at Alex. "I think he soured her on men."

Warmth spread from Kit's toes to her hairline. "That's not true," she snapped.

Jake's gaze darted from Kit to Alex. "Then why ain't you had a fella since?"

She gave Jake her best just-wait-until-I-get-you-alone glare. "You know nothing about my social life while I lived in Europe," she said, avoiding Alex's gaze. "For all you know, I had dozens of boyfriends."

"Not you, Kit." Jake picked up his cane, a satisfied gleam in his pale-blue eyes. "Now if you young folks'll excuse me, I got to get down to the barn."

Alex steadied Jake as he got to his feet. "I've enjoyed your stories. I'd like to hear more of them."

"Anytime, Alex."

After Jake left, Kit forced herself to look at Alex. "You'll have to excuse Jake. He's like a grandfather to me, and sometimes he thinks he knows more about my personal life than he really does. Besides," she said, hoping her voice contained the right degree of casualness, "you could be the married father of a dozen children." The minute she'd said the words, she wanted them back, and Alex's amused look only deepened her embarrassment.

"I'm neither married nor a father, and I'm not offended by Jake's attempt at matchmaking. I think it's amusing."

"Oh?" There was a note of challenge in her tone.

"You're beautiful, all right." His gaze slid over her so intimately she could almost feel it. "Very beautiful," he said with a trace of huskiness in his deep voice, "but it's obvious we have nothing in common."

Kit glared at him belligerently. "Very obvious."

He stared at her for a long moment, cleared his throat, and said, "About . . . Copper King. I'd like to pay you to board him until the end of the month."

Joy gleamed in her eyes, but she extinguished it quickly. She'd have the colt for two more weeks and they'd leave the farm together. She wouldn't have to pass his empty stall or his vacant paddock. "Of course," she said, trying to make her tone matter-of-fact.

"Good." Alex reached into his shirt pocket, took

out a folded check, and handed it to her. "Is that enough?"

Her eyes widened when she saw the amount. "More than enough."

"I want him to have the best."

Kit felt her temper rise. "He's always had the best. All the horses have, and I resent the implication that I could have done more for them. No matter what else . . ." She bit off her words, knowing she'd already said too much.

Alex eyed her narrowly. "No matter what else, *what*?" he prodded.

No matter what else she had to give up, she'd always provided for the horses, she thought, but she'd never say that to Alex or to anyone else. She waved her hand in a careless gesture. "No matter what else I had to do, I always saw that the grooms took good care of the horses. After all, they're such valuable animals." Was that in character? Did she sound pompous and materialistic enough?

"Is that all they are to you? Just investments?"

She hated his judgmental tone and the slight curl of his lip, and anger seared her—a hot, blind fury both with Alex and with her need to sell everything she loved and pretend she wanted it that way. "Isn't that what Copper King is to you? Don't you want him to pay back your investment?" She dropped her hands to her hips, her gaze challenging him. "And think of the stud fees he'll command if he's really good. A million dollars is nothing compared to his potential earnings."

"Then why didn't you keep him?"

The question slammed into her, swiftly draining her anger. For a handful of heartbeats she just stood there, silent. Finally she said, "I—I couldn't. I mean, I didn't . . . want to. I have a life to lead. Keeping Copper King would mean . . . complications."

"I understand," Alex said coldly.

She felt tears well again and she ducked her head to hide them. Pretending interest in the check, she unfolded it with her hands that were a trifle unsteady and glanced at it again. What she saw made her stiffen with shock. "I didn't notice before, but this check is drawn on the Summit Enterprises account. That's the company that bought this place and twenty of my best broodmares."

He eyed her coldly. "No one knows that better than I do."

"You mean you—?"

"I own Summit Enterprises." He glanced around the kitchen, then out the window toward the barns and paddocks. "And in two weeks, I'll own Randall Farm, too."

TWO

Kit stared up at Alex, breathless with shock, then she managed to gasp, "Y-you?"

A swift shadow of pain crossed Alex's face followed instantly by a glittering look so hard and cold it took her breath away. "What's the matter, Ms. Randall? Isn't someone like me good enough to own Randall Farm?" He was silent a moment, and she knew he was containing his anger with an effort. "It *is* ironic, isn't it? Alejandro Menendez, a guy from a dusty little Mexican border town, buys an American racing legend. Tell me, is it true your ancestors' horses raced George Washington's?"

"Yes, but—"

"And after they came to California, the Randalls hired people like me to clean their stables."

Kit's anger leaped and sparked, her gaze narrowing on his face. "My surprise had nothing to do with your origins, *Mr*. Menendez," she said in a voice thin and high with indignation. "I was surprised because no one told me who owned Summit Enterprises. All the papers I received were signed by your accountant."

"J. Wellington Danforth." Alex's lips curved into a tight, humorless smile. "Using Jay's name was quite deliberate. I thought you might cancel the sale if you knew mine."

"Why that's . . . that's the most blatantly prejudiced thing I've ever heard!

His mouth slackened in disbelief. "Me? *Prejudiced*?"

"You say I think of people like you as stablehands, but you think of people like me as snobs. Well, I'm *not* a snob"—she ran her gaze over him—"and it's very clear you're not a stablehand."

He seemed to draw into himself, frowning. "Yes," he said harshly, "very clear." He raked his hand through his already-tumbled hair and stared at her for a diamond-hard instant. "At least . . ." His voice trailed away.

She raised her eyebrows in question, but he didn't continue the thought. Instead, he said, "Now that you've given me something to think about"—he jerked his head in the direction of the stables—"how about showing me my mares?"

She hesitated, looking around the kitchen and mentally running through a list of all she had left to do. She suppressed a sigh, then nodded reluctantly. "All right," she said, and led him out of the kitchen and down the flagstone path to the first of the rambling white stucco barns. "I had the grooms put all your mares into this barn." She hesitated, then added, "It's in better condition than the other one." Avoiding his eyes, she gestured him into the darkness rich with the familiar warm smell of horses and manure. Above the Dutch doors of each of the first ten stalls on either side of the wide center aisle hung magnificent, finely drawn heads. They turned as one in Alex and Kit's direction, ears pricked and nostrils flaring.

She stopped at the first stall and a beautiful blaze-faced chestnut mare craned her neck to nuzzle Kit's hand with rubbery pink-white lips. "This is Scarlet Princess, Copper King's dam. Her sire won the Triple Crown." Kit laughed outright, and Alex smiled in return, his grin a white slash in the gloom of the barn. "I was too young to remember much about the race, but Daddy told me that in the Kentucky Derby, Black Moon Rising was way behind at the head of the stretch. He won by five lengths and in the Preakness and Belmont he . . ."

Realizing her enthusiasm threatened to give her away, Kit waved her hand in an airy gesture and added an uncharacteristic little giggle for good measure. "But I don't suppose you're interested in the trivial details. Just knowing her sire won the Triple Crown is enough to impress your friends."

"I didn't buy the mares to impress my friends. I want to learn all I can about the horses, about the farm, about—everything."

His expression seemed to indicate that "everything" included her. For a crazy instant she wanted to run, but she was pinned there motionless, just looking at him. Finally she dragged her gaze from his, cleared her throat, and turned away. "This . . . this is Scarlet Princess's half sister Moonscape. She's—"

Alex stopped listening. He'd learn about the beautiful gray mare later. Now he found Kit much more intriguing. Just when he thought he had her figured out, she did something completely out of character, like fixing breakfast for Jake or talking enthusiastically about the horses she claimed were complications. Alex frowned at the back of her golden head. She was a puzzle, all right, and he'd always been fascinated by puzzles—especially when one came wrapped in such a beautiful package.

Kit moved to the next stall and he followed close behind, enjoying his view of the heart-shaped bottom that tilted provocatively upward each time she leaned over to check a horse's legs or loosen the cinch on a blanket. Her movements were deft and graceful, her hair gold silk about her face, and her porcelain skin caught the light and focused it, making her face seem luminous in the gloom of the barn. Then she laughed at the antics of one of the horses—a light, flutelike sound that made Alex grin in response. He shook his head to clear it, took a few deep, steadying breaths, and forced his attention back to the horses.

A half hour later, he followed Kit from the cool, shady barn into the sunlight.

"There you are!"

The cultivated, nasal voice came from somewhere to Alex's left and he looked toward it, blinking into the light. A man leaned against one of the posts supporting the wide porch roof. Tall, blond, dressed in a white shirt, tan jodhpurs, and a red-and-white cravat, he looked like the subject of a feature story in *Country Gentleman*. In one black-gloved hand he held the reins of a magnificent gray gelding, in the other, a nasty-looking crop.

Maybe it was the voice, the clothes, the riding crop, the movie-star-handsome face, or all of them together, but Alex decided he didn't like the guy. When Kit smiled at the blond, Alex liked him even less.

"Hello, Blane."

Blane Wentworth. Alex told himself he should have known. He pasted a phony grin on his face and walked forward to be introduced. Wentworth's handshake was as limp as Alex knew it would be, but the guy flashed a dazzling smile. Every tooth in his mouth was capped.

"Mr. . . . Menendez."

"Mr. . . . Wentworth." Alex took perverse pleasure in imitating Blane's slight hesitation, as if Blane's fancy English surname were as unfamiliar to Alex as *Menendez* was to Blane. Alex was pleased to see a spark of irritation in the too-blue eyes. The guy didn't like him, either. Alex's phony smile became real.

"Alex bought Copper King," Kit said.

Blane tilted back his head and looked down his perfect nose at Alex. "I thought as much. My sister told me that a . . . stranger . . . outbid her for the horse, and then she threw a tantrum. Marcella wanted that colt as much as she's ever wanted anything except for a couple of her husbands''—he drew his crop across the toe of one highly polished black boot—''*until* she married them.''

First impression confirmed. The guy really was a bastard. Alex glanced sharply at Kit, who made a helpless gesture and shook her head. He smiled inwardly. Kit didn't like Wentworth, either.

Blane hadn't noticed their silent communication. He smoothed his carefully styled helmet of blond hair and said, ''I know a week is short notice for a formal dance, Kit, but there's one at the club on Saturday. I wonder if you'd attend with me?''

Surprise made Kit hesitate. She hadn't seen Blane for weeks, and someone had told her he was dating a socialite from San Francisco. Well, the woman was certainly welcome to him—*if* she were foolish enough to want him. Kit shifted her feet uncomfortably and wet her lips, trying to frame a polite refusal.

''Kit has already promised to go with me,'' Alex said smoothly, ignoring Kit's surprised look. ''She's going to introduce me to my new neighbors.''

Blane's eyes widened. *''Neighbors?''*

Alex nodded. ''I've bought Randall Farm.''

''You?''

Alex shot Kit a brief, sardonic smile, reminding her of her own reaction when she discovered he was the new owner of the farm. Her hands tightened into fists. She and Blane were *not* alike. They never had been, and she resented Alex's silent suggestion that they were. ''Yes,'' she said quickly, ''Alex. He has great plans for the place. I'm very pleased he bought it.'' She looked straight into Blane's eyes, daring him to argue.

Blane shrugged, his face expressionless, but she detected the anger seething just below his controlled surface. He brushed a strand of hair from her shoulder and looked carefully at her T-shirt and faded jeans. He managed to convey that, on second thought, she wasn't attractive enough to accompany him to the dance. ''Dear Kit, you've always been so . . . different, but I didn't know you'd go so far as to—''

Alex took a menacing stride forward. Blane sidestepped and moved closer to his horse. ''Suit yourself,'' he said, shrugging again. He mounted the gelding, brought the crop down hard on the horse's flank, and the big gray jumped forward.

Wincing each time Blane hit the horse, Kit watched them until they disappeared into the grove of oak trees beyond the paddock, then turned to Alex. ''I'm sorry about that, but please don't judge all the neighbors by Blane.'' She smiled wryly. ''I can truthfully say he's unique.''

''I hope so.'' Alex looked in the direction Blane had gone, his eyes narrowed.

The silence stretched awkwardly between them. Finally Kit sighed and made a throwaway gesture with her left hand. ''I have to get back to the house. I have lots of work to do.''

He turned to her, his expression unreadable. ''What time does the dance start?''

''Nine,'' she said reflexively, ''but it's not necessary, I mean, you don't have to take me.''

"I asked you, didn't I?"

"I thought that was just to get me out of having to go with Blane. You saw I was stuck for an excuse, and—"

"What's the matter, Kit? Are you ashamed to be seen in public with a guy like me?"

"N-no," she stammered, her voice breathless with indignation. "I've already told you I'm not like that!"

"Then prove it."

They locked gazes for an angry moment. She took a deep breath, expelled it, and nodded. "I'll go."

His expression didn't change. "I'll pick you up Saturday at eight-thirty."

The doorbell rang just as Kit finished applying her lipstick. She picked up her blue sequined evening bag, gave a final pat to her hair, which she'd drawn into a loose knot atop her head, and waited until she heard Jake's cheerful greeting to Alex before she headed for the foyer.

Kit had never liked dresses much and she hadn't worn many recently, but tonight the sensuous brush of silk against her legs made her feel glamorous and feminine. Halfway down the hall, she tugged at her low, scooped neckline, wondering again if it weren't a shade too revealing.

When she stepped from the darkened hallway into the lighted foyer, Jake's thin old face lit with a grin, but Alex just looked at her, his expression unreadable. She held his gaze, forced a tiny, tremulous smile, and finally saw his eyes warm. He held out a box containing a single, perfect gardenia. She took the box, stepped to the mirror, and began to pin the flower to the front of her dress.

"No." Alex's beautiful voice was soft, urgent. "Not there." His fingers grazed hers for an electric instant when he took the gardenia from her. He pinned it carefully in her hair and then stepped back to survey her, his gaze lingering, caressing. "You look wonderful."

"So do you." The words were out before she knew she'd said them. His tuxedo was perfectly cut, and his gleaming white shirt made his bronze skin seem darker, his cheekbones higher. Broad-shouldered, narrow-waisted, lean-hipped, he stood with his feet apart, his head bent toward her. Kit wanted to run her fingers through his carefully smoothed hair to restore it to the unruly mass she was used to, but she kept her hands at her sides, the fingers of one digging into the soft fabric of her evening bag.

Behind her, Jake chuckled. "I'll see you young folks out." He moved past them to open the door and, as he did, he winked at Kit. "Have a real good time."

Alex saw the wink and Kit knew he was trying hard to keep the laughter from his voice when he said good night. As they walked toward a silver Mercedes parked in the curving driveway, she said, "Please forgive Jake. He's an incurable romantic."

"You should have taken him to Europe with you. Think of all the fun he'd have had meeting those dozens of boyfriends."

"Uh-huh." Her tone was noncommittal. She refused to confirm or deny the boyfriends. Actually, the "dozens" had been only five in eight years, and none had held her interest for more than a few dates. She'd forgotten most of their names.

When Alex helped her into the car, the touch of his hand on her elbow sent a tongue of flame shooting up her arm. She gave a small, inaudible gasp and frowned into the darkness, trying to quell the flutter of excitement that began in her stomach and spread through her body. She smelled the new leather of the car's interior mixed with the musky fragrance of Alex's aftershave and knew she'd always associate that scent with him. She closed her eyes and saw the sweep of his lashes, his hard profile, the unruly black hair falling across his forehead. Somehow, without realizing until this moment that she had, she'd memorized every detail of him.

Disgusted with herself, she shook her head. Her memories were foolish and futile. In a few days she'd leave Randall Farm and never see Alex again. She tried to distract herself by mentally listing all she had to do before then—the endless details of packing, of making arrangements for Jake, of saying goodbye to friends, of signing the papers turning over Randall Farm to Alex.

But a few seconds later, when Alex lowered himself into the seat beside her and one massive shoulder brushed against hers, she could think only of him. She leaned against the car door to put as much distance as possible between them. She struggled to breathe. The polite social conversation she'd been taught to make deserted her.

Alex had steered the car down the long, winding driveway and onto the main road when he said, "I warn you that I'm not much of a dancer. I worked while other people went to dances."

"Perhaps that's why you're so successful." Kit studied him in the lights of the oncoming cars. Except for his hair, tamed tonight into sleekness, and the expensive clothes, he was exactly as she remembered. She'd hoped he wouldn't be—that she'd magnified him in her mind and the flesh-and-blood reality would be smaller, less magnetic, less . . . desirable. She cleared her throat, balled her hands into determined fists, and promised herself she'd keep the conversation light and escape as early as possible. "You haven't told me what you do," she said, pleased that she'd managed a light, casual tone.

"I invest other people's money."

"That sounds interesting."

Alex's gray gaze flicked over her once before he looked back at the road. "I wouldn't call it that."

Kit gave a soft inner sigh. So much for light conversation. "Then why do you do it?"

Alex turned into the driveway of Riverview Country Club and eased the Mercedes into a parking place near the wood-and-stone clubhouse before he answered. "I won't much longer. I've done it this long so I could afford my dream."

She raised her eyebrows in question. "To own a thoroughbred horse farm?"

A muscle fluttered along his jaw. "To own *Ran-*

dall Farm. I appreciate what it means to American racing and I want to be part of it. You understand that, don't you?''

She bit her lips and looked out the window at the formally dressed couples mounting the wide stone steps to the clubhouse. ''Of course,'' she said, trying to keep the pain from her voice.

Alex raked his fingers through his hair and it fell across his forehead in just the way she remembered. For a few moments he hesitated, as if he were deciding how much to tell her. Finally he said, ''I want to restore the place in memory of your father. He was the finest man I've ever known.''

Shock held her motionless as Alex got out of the car and walked to her side; then a flood of bittersweet memory washed over her and she closed her eyes to keep her tears at bay. Her father had touched so many lives, made so many love him. She shouldn't be surprised that his circle of friends and admirers included Alex. She could only wish that it did not. ''Oh, Daddy,'' she breathed just as Alex reached for the door handle, ''did you have to make him love you, too?''

Riverview Country Club looked splendid that night—a shimmering place pulsing with music and fragrant with flowers. Flattered by the glow from thousands of tiny lights, Kit's friends looked transformed and wonderful.

They were kissing cheeks and being kissed, calling out good-natured jibes and insincere compliments, laughing and teasing as old friends do. Kit stole a slightly worried glance at Alex, but he seemed perfectly at ease.

They threaded their way through the crowd, stopping every few feet so that Kit could introduce Alex to her neighbors, who greeted him politely—and in the case of many of the women, enthusiastically—their impeccable manners firmly in place.

Then Charles Lansing, the elegant, silver-haired president of the Thoroughbred Breeders' Organization, came out of the crowd and swung Kit away in a perfect waltz. She was laughing up at him when she saw, from the corners of her eyes, Alex dancing with Caroline Lansing, Charles's tall, stunning wife. Kit's smile grew wider, and the night was transformed, radiant. The Lansings were sending a clear signal to everyone present that Alex was to become an accepted part of the community. "Thank you, Charles," she said.

He looked down at her, his blue eyes twinkling. "For what?"

She slapped his shoulder playfully. "You know for what."

"We love you, Kit. You brought this man here tonight, and that's good enough for us. The sad part of all this is that in gaining him, we're losing you."

Her smile faded and she fixed her gaze on his shirtfront. "It's necessary."

"I find it hard to imagine Solway without the Randalls." He looked at her hopefully. "You could stay here . . . live in our guest house."

He knew. She'd deluded herself that no one knew about her financial problems, but Charles did. And he must know that they had begun with her father. Charles had been Oliver Randall's best friend. She gazed searchingly at her elegant partner whose face betrayed nothing but concern for her. *Did he know the rest of her father's secret?* "I'm sorry, but I can't."

"Of course you can. You can help with the horses, if you want to. You can—"

"No!" she said too loudly. "I . . . I'm sorry, Charles. I don't mean to be rude, but it's important to me to leave. I have to try to forget, and if I see the farm . . . the horses . . . Copper King"—she looked pleadingly into his round blue eyes, begging him to understand—"it'll just . . . hurt more." Tears stung her eyes. "I have to get away. I just have to."

"All right, but if you ever change your mind, you can always come back to Caroline and me. Kit, I'm—"

The music ended and they were instantly surrounded by friends and neighbors who wanted to say goodbye to her, and whatever Charles was about to say was lost in the babble of voices and laughter. Then Alex was there with his arm lightly around her shoulders and the night was radiant again.

A few minutes later, they drifted away from the group and wandered to the edge of the dance floor. A woman thrust herself between them, placing one bejeweled hand on Alex's arm, the other on Kit's. "How *lovely* you look in that dress, Kit," Marcella Wentworth said. "Blue suits you *so* well."

Marcella wore a form-fitting emerald green sheath. Her beautiful shoulders were bare, along with much of her magnificent bosom. One long leg, sheathed in flesh-colored silk, shone from a thigh-high slit in the clinging, shimmering fabric of her dress. Her flame-like hair was pulled high on her head and caught in a tiara of emeralds and diamonds. Matching earrings glittered at her ears and huge emeralds gleamed at her wrists. She leaned closer to Alex, and one soft breast gently touched his arm as she kissed his cheek. "Ahhhh," she purred, her slanted green cat's eyes narrowing, "my *conqueror*." Her lush, deep voice rose a little. "My brother tells me you've bought Randall Farm. That means we'll be your *closest* neighbors."

Alex gave her a fleeting, formal smile. "So it seems."

If Marcella was disappointed by his unresponsiveness, she didn't show it. She slipped her hand through his arm, dropped the other to Kit's waist, and steered them toward a table at the edge of the dance floor. "You really *must* sit with us. The van Hazeltines couldn't come tonight, so we have two extra seats."

As they approached the table, Blane glowered at Alex, then glanced at the others, doing his best to show it was only out of consideration for them that he extended his hand to Alex. Blane's gaze wandered over Kit, lingering on the valley between her breasts. "As usual, you're the most beautiful woman in the place, Kit."

Resisting the temptation to tug at her bodice, she gave him a practiced, social smile. Blane seldom paid anyone a compliment, and she suspected he'd paid her such an extravagant one to goad Alex. If so, he'd succeeded. Dull red flooded Alex's face and his clear gray eyes went cold and flat.

Marcella waved Alex into the chair beside her. Feeling like a mouse caught between two hungry cats, Kit sat between Alex and Blane.

Marcella pushed her chair closer to Alex's and turned toward him, her back to her date. "Blane said you'll be moving to the farm the first of next month. Perhaps you'll have dinner with me that evening. My brother will be out of town, and I'll be lonely," she said, her eyes and voice full of promise.

Alex's expression didn't change. "I'm sorry, but I plan to do extensive renovations on the farm, and I won't have time for a social life until they're done." Then his expression lightened, his sensuous mouth curved into a half-smile. "A rain check, perhaps?"

Marcella covered his hand with hers. "Of *course*."

"If you'll excuse me . . ." Alex stood and reached out to Kit. "May I have this dance?" Without waiting for her reply, he pulled her to her feet, his expression serious again.

Kit breathed a small sigh of relief as they moved to the dance floor. But as Alex extended his arms to her she felt a breathless tension, a hot white flame in her stomach at the prospect of dancing with him, of being held in his strong arms. Afraid her attraction for him might show in her eyes, she dropped her gaze and stepped into his arms almost woodenly.

Once there, heated blood rushed through her veins and roared through her head. Her lungs seemed paralyzed. Fighting for breath, she tried to maintain some distance between them, but breathless, boneless, she leaned against him, her mind telling her she was making a fool of herself, her body screaming at her not to care.

Something like what she was feeling must have affected Alex, too, because he murmured in Spanish against her hair, gathered her even closer, and folded their arms close to his chest. He kissed her fingertips and his hand was heavy and warm at the base of her spine.

Kit pressed her cheek against him, smelling the fragrance of his aftershave and the fresh scent of his soap, feeling the hardness of his chest beneath the starched fabric of his shirt. His heart thudded against her ear and she knew hers was thudding just as loudly.

They swayed to the slow, sensuous throb of the music, and she was aware of nothing but him. Minutes passed, and she felt Alex's lips against her cheek. She was too vulnerable to him, and she sought a way to distance herself. Finally she said, "How long did you know my father?"

"Twenty-two years—since I was about fifteen," he said quietly.

Surprised, she lifted her head to look at him. "How did you meet?"

"I lived in the Solway area for a few months. He was . . . kind to me. I always regretted not meeting Jake, too, but he was in the East with Black Moon Rising."

She nodded. "That spring and summer was the

best time of Jake's life—and my father's. I was only six, but I felt how excited they were to have a Triple Crown winner—even though I wasn't quite sure what that was.'' She was silent for a moment and then she said, ''It's odd that my father never mentioned you.''

''I said I knew him. I didn't say we were close.'' Sadness shadowed Alex's eyes. ''He was a comparatively young man. I thought there'd be time to get to know him better, but there's never enough time, not for—''

Blane's nasal voice, very close, interrupted him. ''May I cut in?''

She felt Alex stiffen. ''No.''

''It's all right. I don't mind,'' she lied.

''I do.''

''Alex, please. I don't want a scene.''

He hesitated a moment, then released her. ''Of course not. You're the proper Ms. Randall.'' He spun on his heel and walked away, his back stiff with anger.

Feelings grew inside her and she didn't know what to do with them. They were too big, too new. And now he was walking away before they'd even . . . *what*? What did she want from him? A dance? A few kisses? A casual affair? She smiled tightly and shook her head at the impossibility of that. Her feelings for Alex, whatever else they were, could never be casual. Besides, she was leaving, and even if she weren't, they had nothing in common. Alex didn't even know her—only the person she pretended to be. For a while they'd shared a lovely dance and it had ended badly.

That was all, she told herself as she danced with Blane. *That was all.* The words replayed in her head, matching the rhythm of the music.

Blane drew her closer and smiled mockingly. "Like most of his race, Menendez is a volatile fellow."

She looked up at Blane, her eyes narrowing. "He's the same race as we are."

"But he's not like us, is he, Kit?"

"No," she said in a hard, angry voice, "he certainly isn't. He's *earned* what he has."

Blane sighed theatrically. "You're just like the rest of the Randalls—always championing the underdog."

"Only you could think of Alex Menendez as an underdog."

"Oh, he's that, all right." Blane glanced disdainfully in Alex's direction. "He's nothing but a stablehand who's been lucky enough to make some money and buy the farm where he used to work."

Kit stopped dancing and stared at Blane; then the anger she'd been fighting back rose again. "What proof do you have of that?" she asked in a voice loud enough to attract the attention of several other dancers.

"Please, Kit, people are staring. If you must be so . . . undiplomatic, let's go out on the terrace to talk."

She preceded him outside and they stopped by the low wall at the terrace's edge. "I'm listening," she snapped, tapping her foot impatiently.

Blane lighted a cigarette. "Hal Davis, my farm manager, attended the auction and he thought he recognized Menendez, but he couldn't be sure." Blane exhaled slowly, the smoke barely visible in the faint yellow light spilling through the doors. "Then he heard your . . . friend's name and remembered that he was the young troublemaker who worked for us over twenty years ago."

"Troublemaker?"

"Gambling, fighting. Finally he attacked Hal and was fired, of course, but he applied for a job at Randall Farm and your father hired him." Blane shook his head, his lip curling contemptuously. "Oliver was a fool for anyone with a hard-luck story, and I'm sure Menendez concocted a good one."

"My father was the finest, most generous man I've ever known"—her voice cracked with indignation—"and I have no reason to think Alex is a liar."

"Good Lord, Kit! People like Menendez—' "

"What about 'people like Menendez?' " Alex's voice lashed them. He strode forward, his face set in grim lines. He loomed over them, dwarfing Blane, who shrank back from him. "Well?" he demanded, his gaze narrowing on Blane's frightened face.

For a moment Blane's eyes glittered in the soft yellow light. Contact lenses, Kit thought irrelevantly. He's wearing blue-tinted contact lenses. Then Blane shook himself, drawing erect. "I was going to say that people like you can't be trusted, that you—" Blane's Adam's apple bobbed once and he fell silent.

Alex just looked at him. It wasn't an angry or hateful look, just one of the coldest expressions of disdain and disregard she'd ever seen. Then the icy gray gaze turned on her. "I assume you think he's right."

Instantly the focus of her anger switched from Blane to Alex. What right had he to presume he could read her thoughts? What right had he to make her defend herself again? "Of course not!" she said, clenching and unclenching her fists to keep her rage under control. "I've told you I'm not like that!" Head up, eyes flashing, she tried to push past him, but he caught her arm just above the elbow, his fingers digging into her flesh.

"Where are you going?"

"Inside. Home." She tried to yank her arm away, but he held her easily. "I don't know."

"I suggest you make up your mind," he said, his gaze narrow and angry on her face, "because wherever it is, I'm going there, too. I always leave with the woman I came with."

Alex turned on the radio and Chopin spilled into the car's cab, but the molten silver sound did little to dispel the tension between them during the short trip home. As they walked up the path to her front door, the air fairly sizzled with it, and when Alex unlocked her door, handed her the key, and gazed down at her, Kit felt her mouth go dry with nervousness, her heart hammer with it. "Good night," she stammered out, "and . . . thank you."

He took her hand and held it in his own, warmly and firmly. She did not draw it away. "The evening ended badly," he said. "You don't have much to thank me for."

She lifted her shoulders in a tiny shrug. "It seemed like the polite thing to do."

"Do you always do what's polite, like when you danced with Wentworth?"

"I try." She smiled, felt the weight of his stare, and stopped.

"Then wouldn't it be polite to kiss me good night?"

Her chest lifted and fell with the sudden force of her breathing. "I—"

"Wentworth asked you to dance and you *say* you danced with him to be polite. He asked you to go onto the terrace with him, and you did. Now *I'm* asking you to kiss me good night. It's not so different, is it? Just a simple, *polite* good-night kiss?" He placed both hands behind him and leaned against the doorframe, his posture relaxed, his smile—a slash of white in the dark—both mocking and challenging her.

Her heart in her throat, she looked at him uncertainly. He waited, his smile fading.

"I suppose it's a small price to pay to get into my house." Kit's voice was high with tension and she felt a prickling unease that settled at the base of her neck and tightened there.

Alex just looked at her.

She drew closer. His lips parted and his gray eyes glittered under half-closed lids, but he didn't move, didn't seem to breathe.

He was going to make her do it all.

This was her punishment for leaving the dance with Blane. The thought flashed across her mind and she hesitated for a moment, then shoved her doubts aside. *She wanted this. Whatever the reasons for it, whatever Alex's conditions, she wanted this.* She placed her fingertips against his chest and stood on tiptoe to touch his mouth with hers. A tingling thrill of arousal coursed through her. His mouth was so soft, so . . . strangely cherishing.

She was lost.

Her head rang with lightness and her knees and elbows felt loose, detached from her body. For an instant she thought she might faint as she felt his chest, hard under her and his heart, beating with a strong, swift thrumming that seemed to enter her fingers.

His lips at last began to move on hers and, in answer, she leaned her weight against him, her body fitting itself to his. She touched his neck and felt the leap of his pulse, ran her fingers through his thick, silky hair, and caressed the smooth curve of his skull. She rocked her lips on his, a tiny whimper rising in her throat. She wanted his arms around her . . .

Stop! an inner voice screamed. *He doesn't want you! He's just playing a game—a stupid, stupid game of one-upsmanship with Blane!* She struggled for many heartbeats, rational self against feeling self, then, summoning all her willpower, she pushed herself away from Alex. Her entire body felt hot, aching with a strange sensitivity, then cold, bereft, when she moved farther from him. Her lashes fluttered down. She concentrated on slowing her breathing and quieting the thudding of her heart.

He spoke first. "That was . . . unexpected." His

voice seemed lower, tighter, as if pushed with great effort from a place deep in his chest. For long moments he was silent and then he began to laugh—a low, rumbling sound that reverberated in the silence.

She went breathless with anger. "My kissing you was *funny? Funny?*" she repeated, almost unable to understand the meaning of the word. Angry tears smarted in her eyes. She wanted to slap his laughing face, to go into the house and slam the door and never see him again.

"It's just that . . . just that I always wondered what it would be like to be kissed by a princess." His laughter welled again. "Now I know."

THREE

Jake pushed away his cereal bowl, eased back in his chair, and studied Kit. "You're awful irritable this morning. You've been slamming doors and throwing boxes ever since I got here."

"Escrow closes Friday. You know I have to be out of here by then." Seeing Jake's wounded expression, Kit regretted speaking so sharply. "I didn't mean to snap at you. It's not your fault I've let things pile up."

Jake picked up his coffee cup and squinted at her over its rim. "I'll bet that's not what's eating you."

"What else would it be?"

"Alex."

"That's ridiculous." Even to her own ears, her tone was too sharp, her denial too quick.

"Something happened between you at the dance last night that put a burr under your saddle, and you don't want to tell me about it." Jake stretched out his long denim-clad legs and folded his arms across his narrow chest. "I'll just wait right here until you do."

"Look—"

"*You* look. Since your daddy died, I'm the closest thing you got to family, but you don't let me in on anything. You just go about your business pretending nothing's wrong. Shoot, honey, you didn't even tell me you were thinking about selling this place until the day before you put it up for sale."

"I didn't want you to worry."

"What kind of fool do you take me for? I know you and your daddy wouldn't have let the farm run to ruin unless you were having money trouble." Jake set his lips grimly. "And I knew why."

Kit felt as though she'd taken a blow to the midsection. "You . . . knew?"

"Your daddy gave away a lot of money. He liked to live high—"

Kit waited, chewing her lower lip nervously.

"—and after your mama died, he went to pieces. Heck, Evvie hinted about how bad he was in her letters to you, but she said you never seemed to catch her drift."

Kit expelled her breath. Jake didn't know all of it, and she prayed he never would.

Her relief gave way to guilt. If she hadn't been so busy, perhaps she'd have understood some of Evvie's hints. Maybe she'd have come back in time to save the farm.

But she'd spent the four years after her graduation

from college working at some of the best thorough-bred farms in Europe to learn everything she could about bloodlines, training methods, and nutrition. When she returned to Randall Farm, she and her father had planned to work as a team to develop some of the world's finest race horses. It was a dream they'd shared for as long as she could remember. Her mouth twisted into an ironic smile. *The best-laid plans* . . .

She poured Jake another cup of coffee. "I'm sorry I didn't read between the lines of Evvie's letters, but I thought Randall Farm would always be here, as beautiful and smooth-running as ever. Daddy never let on anything was wrong."

Jake made a low-grunting sound, half sympathetic, half disapproving. "Far as I know, he never talked with anybody about his problems. Maybe he wouldn't have died of a stroke when he was only fifty-five if he'd let other people share some of the worry."

"That's not the Randall way."

"It sure as the devil isn't," Jake said, frowning into the depths of his coffee. "Your daddy's pride caused him grief, and yours is making you miserable, too. What's wrong? Forget your pride for a minute and tell old Jake."

Kit shut her eyes, and bright, silvery stars swelled and burst behind her eyelids. Pain knifed through her temple. *Please not now*, she pleaded silently. She had no time for a migraine. The thoughts of all she had to do beat at her and the pain intensified, robbing her of what little will she had to resist Jake's interrogation. "You're right," she said, sighing. "It *is*

Alex. He seems to enjoy playing games with people, manipulating them . . ." *He'd mocked her by calling her a princess. To him, she was an object, a stereotype—not a flesh-and-blood woman with needs . . . and desires.*

Kit's face warmed. She refused to let herself think about those desires. She picked up an empty carton, placed it on the counter, and began to fill it with glasses wrapped in newspaper.

Jake snorted a denial. "If you mean Alex plays games with *you*, I think you're wrong. He likes you, Kit. I saw how he looked at you when he handed you that flower and the way he watches you when you're not looking. That fella can't take his eyes off you."

"You're such a romantic."

"Nothing's wrong with wanting you to have what Evvie and I had. You're like my own daughter, and I want to see you happy before I go." Jake's pale-blue gaze sought hers. "Open up to Alex a little. He's proud, too, and if you act prickly as a porcupine, you'll drive him off."

Jake sipped his coffee, then set down the cup with a clatter. "Why, you probably forgot how to treat a man. I was thinking that last night's date with Alex was the first one you've had since you came home from Europe." Jake raised his thin white eyebrows in question. "That's right, isn't it?"

Slowly she nodded, biting her lip. "But it wasn't a date . . . exactly. I promised him I'd introduce him to the neighbors, and—"

Jake's derisive "Ha!" cut off her words. "So Alex didn't hold your hand or kiss you good night?"

Embarrassment burned in her cheeks.

Jake chuckled. "That's what I thought."

She searched for a way to change the subject. "Alex knew my father," she said. "He wants to restore the farm in Daddy's memory."

Jake's eyes widened in surprise, then he frowned thoughtfully and, after a moment's hesitation, nodded. "I'm real glad about that. Seems like the next best thing to having you keep the place." He leaned back in his chair, hooked his thumbs into his belt, and squinted out the window into the bright morning sun. "You know, I've been thinking how funny it'll seem not to have a Randall on the farm."

"That can't be helped."

"Sure it can. Under the terms of the sale, one of us has to stay and help out Alex for the first six months. I think it should be you." Jake anticipated her protest and lifted a restraining hand. "I could get my own little place in Solway. I'd be close enough to stop by and help you and the boys."

Kit shook her head determinedly. "We agreed you'd stay. I know you want to, and the work won't be demanding."

"But—"

Hands on hips, chin thrust out in what her mother had laughingly called the "Randall pose," Kit said, "Let's not argue. You stay and I leave. That's final." Lord, how her head hurt! She blinked several times, trying to clear her vision. "Look at it from my point of view," she said more gently. "I love the place, but I won't own it anymore. I need to make a break that's quick and final. Hanging around will only hurt more."

She saw the sad shadow in Jake's eyes and added more brightly, "Besides, I'm used to giving orders around here. I don't think I could learn to take them."

The grooves beside Jake's mouth deepened. "That's just your pride talking again. You got to learn to bend a little."

"I'd be the first Randall who did." She smiled ironically. Last night, she'd let Alex humiliate her. If that was what "bending a little" meant, she wanted no part of it.

"All right," Jake muttered, "I'll stay, but I don't have to like it."

"You'll stay and you'll *love* it. You're going to have a wonderful time watching Randall Farm become beautiful again and telling Alex everything you know about the place."

She heard a knock and looked toward the door, expecting one of the grooms, but Alex stood in the doorway. "I thought you'd be up," he said, grinning at Jake. "How's breakfast?"

"Not so bad a plateful of steak and eggs wouldn't cure it." Jake drained his coffee. "You're up early again this morning."

An expression Kit hadn't seen before crossed Alex's face—a soft, almost shy, look. "I'm sorry to make a nuisance of myself. I can't seem to stay away."

"You're not a nuisance. On Friday, it'll all be

yours anyway.'' Jake got up slowly. "Why don't you sit yourself down and have some coffee? I promised Miguel and the boys I'd show them how to make my special poultice for Scarlet Princess. She hit her knee and the swelling hasn't gone down as fast as I figured it would.''

"May I help?''

Jake shook his head and waved dismissively. "I'll have plenty of help.''

Kit studied Jake as carefully as her pounding head and out-of-focus vision would allow. He'd said nothing about Scarlet Princess's having a swollen knee, and he wore that Mona Lisa half-smile he always got when he was lying. He was making an excuse to leave her alone with Alex.

The room seemed to tilt and she grabbed the edge of the counter to steady herself. She didn't want Jake's matchmaking and she certainly didn't want to be alone with Alex. She wanted to go back to bed, to press cold compresses to her temples, to shut out the light, and perhaps, if she were lucky, to sleep.

Jake left, banging the door, or to her sensitized ears it seemed to bang. She forced herself to stand straight, picked up the coffeepot, and extended it to Alex, raising her eyebrows in question. He held out a cup she'd left on the counter to be packed. The glass pot wavered as she poured and the coffee splashed onto Alex's hand. Startled, she jerked back the pot and shattered it against the counter, then stared uncomprehendingly from the spilled coffee and glass shards on the floor to the handle of the pot in her hand. A white light exploded in her head and she leaned limply against a cabinet.

Alex took the handle of the pot, placed it in the sink, and rested his hands on her shoulders. "What's wrong?"

"Nothing. I'll be fine." She closed her eyes.

"Do you have a headache?"

"A migraine," she admitted reluctantly. "I seem to be getting a lot of them lately."

"Moving is stressful, even for someone as eager to get on with her life as you are." He tightened his grip on her shoulders. "May I help?"

"There's nothing you can do." She swayed slightly.

"I wonder how I knew you'd say that?" He dropped his hands to her waist to steady her and she felt the heat from his body strike through her thin cotton T-shirt. "You're twenty-seven, aren't you, Kit?"

"Twenty-eight."

"In those twenty-eight years, have you ever asked anyone for help?"

Anger overrode her pain. His question was a continuation of her conversation with Jake, and she was tired of it. What was wrong with refusing to burden other people with her problems? If she were a man, Alex would admire her independence. "My parents and grandparents helped me, and so did Jake and Evvie."

"That isn't my question. I want to know if you've ever *asked* for help. There's a difference."

Dust motes danced crazily in a bar of too-bright light. "Not that I remember."

"I thought not." Kit felt him move closer and opened startled eyes when he lifted her into his arms and cradled her against him. "Which way to your bedroom?"

"What?"

"Don't sound so shocked. I'm not going to force myself on you. I'm going to see that you rest. Which way is it?"

"Down the hall, the last door to the right. But this isn't—"

"Necessary. I know."

Held high above the floor, she lay stiffly in his arms, resisting her desire to cuddle against him, to run her fingers through his thick, tumbled hair. Instead, she concentrated on trying to relieve the pain of the rockets exploding in her head, of the hundreds of sledgehammers beating against her skull.

She barely felt the softness of the mattress against her back when Alex laid her on it and began to pull off her boots. She winced when they hit the floor. Vaguely she knew he'd gone to the bathroom and turned on a faucet. Moments later, the bed sagging under his weight, he pressed a cold towel to her forehead. "Relax. I'm going to massage your temples." He pulled her head onto his lap and began a slow, circular movement of his fingers.

At first, Kit resisted him, lying stiffly on his lap, the muscles of her neck and shoulders tense and knotted. Then she felt her cheeks flush, her entire body warm and gradually relax. They were so close she could feel the intake of his breath, the sinewy strength of his thighs beneath her head, the great bulk of his torso against her cheek, smell his scent. *Years*. It had been years since she'd felt so safe, so protected, so . . . cherished.

"Sleep now," Alex whispered. "I'll take care of everything."

She smiled faintly. It felt good to be cared for . . . just this once.

Minutes later, she slept.

Kit woke in the late afternoon, her headache gone. She lay still, listening to the silence of the big old house, and let thoughts of Alex came flooding back. Abruptly she sat up. She couldn't afford to think too much about him or to let him become a bigger part of her life than he already was. She frowned into the gloom. For years she'd pretended to have no needs. Now Alex had come along and she was a bundle of needs and she didn't like it. It felt too much like weakness. She got up and padded barefoot into the kitchen.

Alex sat at the table in the middle of the room, a book propped in front of him. Smiling, he pulled out a chair for her. "I was going to let you sleep a while longer before I called you for dinner. There are potatoes baking and I was about to throw some steaks onto the grill."

Tight-lipped, she surveyed the room. The mess on the counter had been cleared away, and many newly filled cartons had been packed and stacked neatly against the walls. "You've been busy," Kit said, not trying to keep the edge from her tone.

"As long as I was here, I thought I'd help out a little."

"This is more than a little."

Alex closed his book with a snap. "You don't like it."

"Are you trying to see that I'm out on Friday even if you have to move me out yourself? I assure you I'll make the deadline, even without your help."

"Did you expect me to sit around all day waiting for you to wake up?" he asked harshly, rising to tower over her.

"I expected you to go home, or to work, or wherever you go—not to move me out of my home. It's . . . presumptuous."

Alex dropped his hands onto her shoulders. "Oh, I'm presumptuous all right, lady. Let me show you just how much."

His lips descended on hers. She couldn't breathe, couldn't move. For a moment she struggled in his grasp, then clung helplessly to him while his hands roamed over her body and his lips caressed her mouth.

She responded to his dominance with tiny, tentative gestures—brushes of her fingers against his cheek, flutterings of her tongue inside his mouth. His hand cupped her breast and she moaned with surprise and delight, a melting sweetness coursing through her. She felt him tremble, heard his answering groan, and, emboldened, matched the intensity of his kisses. She felt the hard column of his manhood pressed against her and smiled against his lips, proud of her power. At that instant, he dragged his lips from hers and moved away from her. Slowly she opened her eyes. His face was flushed with desire, and even though he was no longer touching her, their intimacy thickened the air between them.

Alex began to speak, cleared his throat, and began again. "Perhaps I'm not as presumptuous as I . . . we . . . thought," he said thickly, his gaze dropping to her swollen lips.

She inhaled sharply, then said, "Perhaps not, but this won't—it *can't*—happen again."

He looked at her questioningly.

"You think of me as a shallow, careless woman— a jetsetter who's spent a large part of her life traveling in Europe and attending parties, but that stereotype doesn't entirely fit me."

"Oh?"

She looked at him carefully, cool, trying to be detached. "I don't have casual affairs." *Or any other kind, for that matter. Until now, I haven't even been tempted.*

He set his lips in a tight smile and said, "What makes you think it would be casual?"

"Time. I'm leaving Friday as soon as we complete the paperwork."

"You don't have to."

She tried to smile, felt the weight of his stare, and stopped. "Perhaps not, but I want to." *I want to blot out the memories of you, of the farm, of my failure, and I need to start as soon as I can.*

His gaze searched hers, then he gave a what-can-I-do shrug. "Then we'll see each other just twice more."

"Twice?"

"Have you forgotten about Wednesday? That's the day I make my final inspection of the place before escrow closes. I expect you to show me every inch of the property. I'll bring a picnic lunch. You supply the horses." He tilted up her face, his thumb caressing the tiny dimple on her chin. "Remember," he said, and walked out, closing the door softly behind him.

Still shaken, she stared at the closed door for long moments until the sharp buzz of the oven timer reminded her they'd forgotten dinner.

On Wednesday morning Kit watched a bright-yellow moving van lumber down her driveway carrying her household goods to storage. She'd kept only a few things—her father's desk, her parents' huge four-poster, the contents of the library and kitchen, and her father's diaries and papers, including the farm records that would soon belong to Alex.

She put the cartons containing the records and her father's papers and journals into the trunk of her car. She'd sort through them in the next couple of days while she stayed at Jake's and give the records to Alex when escrow closed. By midmorning Friday, she'd be on her way to . . . *where*? She drew her brows together thoughtfully. Perhaps she'd stay at the old inn at Big Sur where she and her family had vacationed when she was a child. Once there, she'd relax for a days days and then call her acquaintances in the thoroughbred business. Maybe she could find a job managing a farm in the East or in Europe, where she wasn't so well known.

She looked down the steeply sloping lawn past the overgrown flower beds and the cool, dappled shade of the oak trees. From this distance, the green paddocks surrounded by brown, four-board fences looked as they had in her childhood, immaculate and perfect. If she kept her gaze focused into the distance, she could almost fool herself into believing that nothing had happened.

But something *had* happened to her dream and her future and she had to put all this behind her. She gave a long, shuddering sigh. Soon Jake would be her last, tenuous link to this place, and after his death, she'd never see it again. She'd spend the rest of her life a continent or half a world away.

She heard a car engine and turned as Alex stopped the Mercedes in front of the house. He got out, reached inside to remove several small boxes, and strode toward her. Gray jodhpurs clung to his muscular legs and slim hips like a second skin and a white shirt, its sleeves rolled to his elbows, stretched tautly over his massive shoulders and upper arms. He was a powerful, looming, vital presence, and as he walked toward her, she straightened, tensed, and drew her defenses around her like a shield.

Smiling, he stopped in front of her. "Well? Do I pass inspection?"

"Yes." Embarrassed that he'd commented on her inspection, she dropped her gaze to his boots. They were black, handmade, and so fine that her own scuffed boots looked even shabbier by comparison.

She smiled an ironic, inner smile. Her boots did go well with her patched tan jodhpurs and faded plaid shirt, though. They were all equally old and scruffy.

She looked straight into Alex's mesmerizing gray eyes and her heart rate doubled. "What's . . . in the boxes?"

"Our lunch. I brought it with me from San Francisco when I flew my plane down this morning. My adoptive aunt keeps house for me and she worked over it long and tenderly. She thinks I don't pay attention to what I eat, that I work too much, and that I don't get enough sleep."

"Is she right?"

"Yes, I'm afraid she is, but once I've completed the sale of Summit Enterprises and finished renovating the farm, I'll have a lot more time."

"What will you do with all of it?"

Alex looked at her for a long moment. "Acquiring Randall Farm wasn't just a whim, Kit. I'm going to run it with the kind of dedication and love your father and grandfather had."

And I have, too, Kit thought, and changed the subject. "I've had Miguel saddle Scarlet Princess for me and Moonscape for you. I hope you like her."

Alex followed Kit to where the mares were tied and put the boxes into Moonscape's saddlebags. Just before he mounted he said, "I see that Scarlet Princess has recovered from her swollen knee. Jake whips up a miraculous poultice. Remind me to ask him for his formula."

Kit bent to check Scarlet Princess's cinch. "I'm afraid Jake will never give up trying to play Cupid,

even if the people he tries to pair up are totally in-
compatible.'' She let the words *like we are* hang in
the air between them, and without looking at Alex,
mounted her mare and rode toward the steep rutted
trail leading to the northern boundary of Randall
Farm.

She stole a glance at him over her shoulder. Alex
was an excellent rider and she felt guilty that she
hadn't offered him a more spirited horse. She gave
a small inner shrug. Beginning on Friday Alex could
ride any horse he chose.

She guided Scarlet Princess through a narrow pas-
sage between two enormous granite outcroppings,
came into the open, and felt a hot breeze carrying
the faint scent of the Pacific that lay behind her. To
the north and east golden brown foothills shouldered
their way to the horizon. Below her, in a small cup
of valley, Randall Farm lay green and somnolent in
the midday heat. *It's the last time,* she thought, *the
last time I'll make this ride, the last time I'll look
down on the farm.* Tears started, hot and stinging
and sudden, but she blinked them away.

''I'm sorry I didn't offer you a livelier horse,''
Kit said when she and Alex had reached a wide, flat
place next to the trail with a clear view of Wentworth
Farm. She slid off Scarlet Princess and led the mare
into the dense shade of an oak.

Alex dismounted, too. ''I like Moonscape. She's
a thoughtful horse, even if she is slow.''

''She was fast when she was on the track, but if
you were the middle-aged parent of four children,
you'd slow down, too.''

"I think that would be a good idea."

"What?"

"To slow down in middle age and to be the father of four."

"You don't seem the type," she said as his gaze locked with hers.

"You don't know me well enough to know what type I am"—Alex carefully tethered the mare and began to remove the boxes from her saddlebags— "but I suspect you think children are complications, like the farm and the horses."

The hot breeze ruffled Alex's hair and Kit pictured a small boy with the same midnight hair and haunting long-lashed gray eyes. He'd be a bright, handsome child, one that . . . she shut off the thought. She untied a blanket from behind her saddle and spread it on the ground in the shade. "I've never thought about children," she said, accompanying her casual tone with a careless shrug.

She took two boxes from Alex, opened them, and began to lay out their contents. "I'm starving. I got up earlier than usual to supervise the movers and I didn't have breakfast," she said, wondering if her abrupt change of subject was too obvious.

Alex studied her narrowly for a moment, shrugged, and said, "I guess that means Jake didn't get his breakfast, either."

"Miguel fixed it for him, but he didn't eat much. I'm worried about him."

Alex sat down on the blanket and unwrapped the food—chicken, a variety of salads, homemade bread and chocolate cake—enough to feed a pack of hungry

Boy Scouts. "Jake's been sick and he's had a lot of stress. He's worked for the Randalls all his life and getting used to me will be hard for him, but he'll be all right."

"I wish I could be sure of that," Kit said between bites of honeyed chicken, light as air, that seemed to dissolve in her mouth. "He's lived on the farm forty years, and moving bothers him more than he'll admit." Kit took a long, slow swallow of the lemonade Alex poured for her and dabbed her mouth nervously with a paper napkin. "I wonder if I could ask a favor."

His mouth full of potato salad, Alex could only nod.

"For the six months he'll work for you, Jake will live rent free in his old house on the property. After that, he'll need a place to live. I'd like to rent his house from you for as long as he's able to live by himself." Kit knew her request would seem out of character, but she'd have to risk it. At Jake's age and in his fragile condition, moving from the place he loved might kill him.

"Of course he can stay, but I won't accept any rent from you."

Kit frowned. "He can't afford to pay much himself."

"You miss the point. I don't want money from either of you. The house is Jake's reward for a lifetime of faithful service to the Randalls."

Kit put down her paper plate, still heavy with food. "It's not up to you to reward Jake for his service to my family. That's my responsibility."

Alex's gray eyes were unwavering. "Do you want Jake to have the house?"

"Yes, but—"

"Then you'll have to accept my terms."

Kit sighed inwardly. She didn't like being obligated to Alex, but she had no choice. Tight-lipped, she nodded. "Thank you." She forced a smile. "You see? I did ask for help after all."

"For Jake, not for yourself." Alex poked at his potato salad with a plastic fork, then lifted his head to frown at her. "But that's what I expected."

She wiped her greasy fingers on her napkin. "I'm consistent, anyway."

"Your pride, what I think of as your stubborn independence—that's consistent." His keen gaze measured her, probing her, searching for something and appearing not to find it. He sighed and ran his fingers through his tumbled hair. "The rest is a mass of contradictions. You're a bewildering woman.

"Mmm," she said teasingly, "I think of myself as rather straightforward."

"You're mixing us up. I'm the straightforward one." His tone matched hers, but he gave her a searching look. "There are layers and layers to you."

She ignored his last words with their implied question and said swiftly, "Well, if you're so forthright, tell me how you met my father."

"There's no great mystery about it. I dropped out of high school and came to this area because I'd heard jobs were available at the horse farms. My first job was down there." He pointed in the direction of

Wentworth Farm, his lip curling with distaste. "I didn't last long. One day I saw a man mistreating a horse and I hit the guy. He happened to be the manager and he fired me on the spot."

"Hal Davis is a first-class bastard."

"He's still there, is he?"

"For twenty-five years now. Together he and Blane and Blane's father before them have ruined a lot of good horses."

"Why hasn't something been done about them?"

Kit looked straight ahead at the ostentatious pink brick buildings of Wentworth Farm, and shook her head. "I think people are afraid of Hal Davis. He's stupid, so he can't be reasoned with, and he has a terrible temper."

"By anybody's measure. The day he fired me, I walked over to Randall Farm and asked your father for a job. I lied about my age and he pretended to believe me." Alex settled his broad shoulders against the trunk of the oak, his lunch momentarily forgotten. "I worked for Oliver until he convinced me to go back to school. He said if I did well, he'd send me to college."

Kit nodded slowly. "I'm not surprised," she said, her voice husky. "My father was a wonderfully generous man." *Even after he couldn't afford to be generous anymore.* She sat still for a long time, her expression thoughtful. "And did you?" she finally asked.

Alex was as lost in thought as she had been, and he looked confused for a moment. "Did I what?"

"Go back to school and do well."

He nodded. "After I graduated from high school your father sent me to Stanford." Alex shook his head wonderingly. "He never mentioned it to anyone."

Kit's lips trembled. "Daddy always believed that he had an obligation to help others, but he never took any credit. He didn't help out for praise, but because he thought it was the right thing to do." She swung her gaze to Alex's. "He must have been especially proud of you. Stanford was his alma mater."

"I *hope* he was proud of me," Alex said in a voice deep with emotion. "Buying Randall Farm was my way of repaying him for all he'd done for me. I knew he wouldn't want strangers to own it." Alex looked at her accusingly.

Kit's face froze into a bleak emptiness. "No," she said, stung, her guilt rushing back, "but he wouldn't want me to keep the farm if owning it was a burden."

"You could have hired a manager . . . saved it for your children."

A tremor ran through her. "But I didn't, and now it's too late." She put out a hand, a barrier to stop his voice. "I don't want to discuss it anymore."

"Look at me," he said roughly, but she shook her head, gazing unseeing toward the distant ocean. "You sold your birthright, Kit."

Something cracked and shifted inside her, but she couldn't show remorse. Instead, she took refuge in anger. Leaping up, she spilled the lemonade and clumsily planted a booted foot on her plate. "You grew up poor," she said in a trembling voice. "How could you know what a burden owning Randall Farm can be? It's a legend, a piece of racing history. People were always watching, comparing me with my father and grandfather." Her voice rose. "Maybe I couldn't take the pressure."

"You're not a coward," he said softly. "I know that much about you."

"You know a lot less about me than you think you do."

He rose, put his hands on her shoulders, and gazed searchingly into her eyes. "I *want* to know about you, though."

"Why? So you can figure out how a fine man like my father managed to raise a daughter who'd sell everything he valued?" She let anger shoot through her like a flame. "Well, I don't want you to know me. I don't have to explain myself to anyone, least of all to you."

She jerked away from him, marched over to Scarlet Princess, and mounted the mare. Kit's hands shook on the reins, and the horse, sensing her anger, paced nervously. Alex reached for the reins, but Kit jerked the mare away from him, sending a shower of stones down the steep trail behind her.

"You agreed to show me the property lines."

"I didn't agree to have you sit in judgment of me, to remind me—" Her breath stopped and she stared down at him, her chest heaving. "Over there"—she pointed to a spot next to a granite outcropping—"is the northwest property stake. Once you find that, the line is easy to follow." She turned the mare and sent her down the trail toward home.

When Kit reached the flat, cultivated area of the farm, she let the Scarlet Princess canter toward the barns. The soothing rhythm of the horse took away the last of her anger. After all, Alex had said only what she'd told herself many times. He was out of line to say it, but she understood the love that motivated him. "You were some kind of man, Daddy," she said, her words caught and flung back at her by the breeze.

She slowed the mare. She'd never tell Alex that Oliver Randall had been less than perfect. She'd let Alex maintain the illusion he'd built his life on. Her silence was all she could give him.

She approached the barn, frowning when she saw a knot of shouting, gesturing men standing near one of the barns. Miguel detached himself from the group and ran toward her. She yanked the reins and Scarlet Princess skidded to a stop. "What's wrong?"

Miguel lifted his frightened face to look wildly at her. "It's Jake! He's had another heart attack!" he shouted, his voice cracking.

_____ FOUR _____

The aqua-and-mauve waiting room of the intensive care unit looked like a living room, and the elegant silver-haired woman serving coffee resembled Kit's grandmother, but Kit still hated hospitals. She breathed slowly and deeply, trying to force her heartbeat back to normal. She accepted a Styrofoam cup of coffee, refused sugar and cream, and settled into a deep, comfortable chair. She sipped the coffee, not tasting it, but the familiar act comforted her and the heat from the cup warmed her hands.

Why were hospitals always so cold, even in the middle of summer? She rested her head against the chairback and closed her eyes, feeling sudden tears prickle her eyelids. Jake couldn't die! He was all she had left. She clenched her teeth to keep them from chattering. The room wasn't *that* cold, but she was, deep down inside. She felt someone standing beside her chair and opened her eyes.

"How is he?" Alex asked.

She turned to look up at him and her neck locked painfully. "I don't know."

He pulled her to her feet and wrapped his arms around her, letting his warmth envelop her. Slowly her galloping heartbeat settled into a more livable rhythm. "Jake loves life and he'll fight hard to hang onto it. Don't give up on him," Alex said.

She saw sorrow and worry in Alex's eyes and knew that he was trying to convince them both that Jake would be all right. Alex genuinely liked the old man and she knew that if he lived, Jake would always have a home at Randall Farm.

Alex led her to a sofa and sat beside her. "Neck stiff?" he asked softly. When she nodded, he turned her away from him and began to massage the base of her neck. She felt the stiffness lessen, her body loosen and soften, her eyelids grow leaden. *Magic*, she thought. *His fingers, his hands, are magic.* "Try to rest," he whispered. "I'll wake you if there's any news."

"I can't rest. I keep thinking what's happened to Jake is my fault. He had his first heart attack two days after I told him I was selling the farm, and now this . . ." *But I had no choice, old friend. I had no choice.*

Alex squeezed her hand. "Try not to be so hard on yourself. Jake wouldn't blame you."

"I know that," she said softly, "but I blame myself."

"Ms. Randall? I'm Dr. Miller." The thick carpeting had muffled the doctor's footsteps and now he towered over her, an almost impossibly tall, pencil-thin man with receding red hair and thousands of freckles blooming on his pale face. She jumped to her feet and squared her shoulders, preparing herself for the worst, but afraid to hear it.

He smiled reassuringly, his mild hazel eyes narrowing behind the glasses that had begun to slip down his bony nose. "Mr. Blaylock is stable. We thought we'd lost him a couple of times, but he wouldn't give up. He's quite a fighter."

"Will he live?"

"We'll know in the next twenty-four hours." The doctor shoved his glasses back onto the bridge of his nose with a long, freckled forefinger and studied her, his eyes huge behind the thick lenses. "Why don't you go home and get some rest? We'll call you if there's any change in his condition."

"I'm staying here."

He nodded. "I'll get you a room." He loped to the reception desk and picked up a telephone.

"There's no reason for you to stay, too," Kit said, sitting down next to Alex again.

"I haven't had many friends in my life, and even though I've known him just a short time, I consider Jake one of them. I'm staying." The stubborn set of Alex's jaw warned her not to argue.

For a moment after she woke, Kit couldn't remember where she was, but then the antiseptic smell of the hospital brought everything back. Her eyes sprang open and she stared into the gloom, her anxiety about Jake returning in a rush. She assured herself that a nurse would have awakened her if anything had happened to him, and her heartbeat began to return to normal.

Her head felt heavy, her eyelids leaden. Dr. Miller's sedative, taken under protest, had some unexpected side effects. She pressed her fingertips to her temples and massaged them until the heavy, drowsy feeling began to dissipate.

A bar of sunlight thrusting through a crack between the draperies showed her Alex's massive form slumped in a chair, his long legs stretched in front of him. He seemed to be asleep. She sat up and frowned at her watch, but the illuminated dial remained out of focus.

Alex's voice startled her. "It's almost ten."

"*Ten*? In the *morning*?"

"You slept almost eighteen hours. The doctor's sedative could have felled one of the horses."

Kit threw her legs over the side of the bed—or tried to. They moved much slower than she expected. "Jake—"

"He's all right. I've checked on him several times."

Kit shuddered as her stocking feet hit the cold floor. She pushed back her hair, fumbled for her boots, and blinked when Alex opened the draperies. "I haven't slept this late since high school."

"You haven't?" Alex crossed the room to stand by the bed. He took her hand and inspected her calloused palm, then ran his thumb over her broken nails. "Most rich girls sleep late and have soft hands." He eyed her patched jodhpurs and scuffed boots. "And they dress better than you do."

She snatched back her hand. "I'm the exception. A rich eccentric, that's me," she snapped defensively.

"I wonder."

During an awkward silence, Kit pulled on her boots, grateful for the thick curtain of hair that hid her face from Alex's probing gaze. She had to get away from him. She couldn't maintain the pretense much longer. She wasn't used to lying, and she was bad at it.

She jumped at a knock and stared at the door as it was pushed open, a knot of fear in her stomach. The doctor's thin face was lit with a boyish smile. "Mr. Blaylock is amazing," he said. "He's awake and asking for you. He swears he's going back to steak and eggs because the women and kids' food you've been feeding him doesn't work."

Kit paused outside the heavy glass door to the escrow office and adjusted the jacket of her ivory silk suit to cover the smudge Copper King's nose had left on her blouse. She patted her hair, drawn into a tight knot at the back of her neck, pulled open the door, and stepped inside.

Once inside the office, her courage failed her. She walked forward on legs suddenly gone weak, smiling mechanically at the pretty receptionist. Kit felt vague and unfocused. A telephone rang, but the sound was muted. A couple talked at the far end of the room, but their words didn't register. When the receptionist led her into a large conference room with a rectangular mahogany table in the middle, Kit saw the room and its occupants through a haze.

Alex and another man—the escrow officer, she supposed—stood when she entered. Alex wore what her father had always referred to as "corporate armor"—gray suit, white shirt with heavy gold cufflinks, and a red-and-gray silk tie. A matching handkerchief projected just the right distance above his breast pocket, and his newly trimmed hair clung to his head in a sleek, quasi-military style. He was remote, almost inaccessible, his handshake brief and firm.

The other man was paunchy, balding, blue-suited, and about forty. Alex introduced him, but his name didn't register. Kit sat down opposite Alex, rested her hands in her lap, and stared at the papers the escrow officer placed in front of her. She tried to read, but the words made no sense. The hazy, disembodied feeling persisted. She guessed it was shock— her mind's way of protecting itself against a loss almost too terrible to bear.

She roused herself with an effort. *Soon*, she told herself firmly. Just a few more minutes and she'd be through the worst. After Jake was out of the hospital, she'd start her new life—one where she wouldn't have to lie or pretend to be calm when she felt like screaming.

She forced herself to concentrate on the jumble of words before her. One phrase stood out: "Katherine Howard Randall agrees to transfer ownership of the property described hereinafter . . .'' The stark legal language that followed described her home.

Kit interlaced her fingers and squeezed them together so tightly her knuckles whitened. After she read each page, she reached out quickly to turn to the next, hoping Alex wouldn't notice her trembling. He finished reading before she did, and when she looked up, his gaze was fastened on her. ''Everything seems to be in order,'' she said through dry lips. A line on the last page required her signature. She fumbled for a pen the escrow officer extended and held it poised above the page.

''Just a minute.'' Alex's voice cut through the air like a whiplash.

Kit started. ''What's the matter?''

''You seem to have skipped over an essential part of the agreement. Look at page four.'' He flipped through his copy, found the page, and skimmed it. ''Paragraph five states that you are to provide a trainer for the horses for six months.''

Kit resented Alex's imperious tone and the arrogant tilt of his head. She raised her chin and met his gaze squarely, her eyes narrowing. ''I spoke with your agent about that. She said you agreed Jake was acceptable in that position.''

''Jake is sick.''

''There's only Copper King to train and Jake will be better soon.'' She heard the escrow officer shift in his chair.

''But Copper King is a very expensive horse. To get back my investment in him, I need him on the track as soon as possible. As for Jake—he'll get better, but how *soon* is anybody's guess. I know he won't be well enough to help me now, when I need him most.''

Kit shrugged, pretending a nonchalance she didn't feel. ''Miguel knows a lot about training. He'll help until Jake can take over.''

''Miguel isn't a trainer. You and Jake are the two qualified trainers at Randall Farm. Jake is incapacitated. That leaves you.''

Kit shook her head. ''I can't do it. Jake's heart attack has already delayed my plans. I'm leaving here as soon as he's out of the hospital and settled at home.''

Alex pinned her with his hard gray gaze, letting the silence stretch out between them. ''Then the deal is off.'' He threw down his pen and it skittered off the table.

Determined not to let her fear show, Kit fought to keep her face expressionless. After the farm's debts were paid, she wouldn't realize much money from the sale, but at least she'd avoid bankruptcy. If Alex backed out, she'd have no choice but to file chapter eleven. Some enterprising reporter might investigate the reasons for the bankruptcy. He'd learn about her father . . . Her breath shortened and hammers began to pound her temples again.

If she agreed to stay on as the colt's trainer, she'd be an employee on the farm she'd once owned. She'd be forced into daily contact with Alex. He was already asking probing questions, battering her defenses. What would he learn if she stayed another six months?

Gloomily, she stared down at her hands, then out the window at the hot, bright day. Finally she looked at Alex. "All right," she said, "you've got yourself a trainer."

Kit looked out the window of the stifling room under the eaves at Jake's house and reminded herself that everything she saw belonged to Alex. She smiled grimly. In a way, she belonged to him, too, because she wasn't free to leave. For the first time in her life, she felt trapped on Randall Farm.

She walked to the narrow bed heaped with her clothes, picked up some dresses, and began to hang them in the closet. When she put everything away, the room would seem larger, but she'd still feel crowded in the tiny space. Alex had offered to let her stay in the main house until he began to remodel it, but she'd refused. She could avoid him more effectively here, and when Jake came home from the hospital, he'd be a buffer between them. *If* he chose to act as a buffer, she thought gloomily. So far, he'd been intent on throwing them together.

She picked up the dress she'd worn to the dance and let the delicate material drift through her fingers, then held the dress against her cheek. The silky fabric still smelled faintly of Alex. Filled with nostalgia and longing, she closed her eyes, realized the trap she was letting herself fall into, and jerked them open. She marched to the closet and thrust the dress inside, followed it with her other dresses, and shut the closet door.

She had to start thinking of Alex as her employer.

She had to be cool, professional, and distant. She'd always been disciplined. Once she'd identified a goal, she'd moved toward it with a singlemindedness that surprised everyone who knew her. She'd do that again.

Hands on hips, Kit surveyed the small, shabby room without enthusiasm. With most of her clothes put away, it *did* look larger, though, and tomorrow she'd drive into Solway for a new bedspread and curtains.

The thought of buying something new momentarily cheered her. Maybe she'd even paint the room. "What do you think of that, Matilda?" she asked Jake's old cat, who eyed her sleepily from atop a stack of sweaters. "White walls would make this room look a lot larger, wouldn't they?"

Matilda stretched and began to purr. From a distant paddock, Copper King whinnied and Kit glanced guiltily at the bedside clock. It was two hours past the time when he usually got his carrots. Jake's illness had disrupted the farm's schedule, and horses liked the security of a routine.

Five minutes later, Kit stood by the paddock fence and extended a carrot to Copper King. "I know you haven't been getting as much attention as usual," she crooned to the colt, "but I promise that will change. Tomorrow I'll make up a new schedule so the men will have time to visit Jake and get their work done, too." *If* that was one of her duties. She wasn't sure what Alex wanted her to do or if he'd give her any freedom to use her own judgment.

Copper King raised his head and pricked his ears, his nostrils flaring. Kit followed the colt's gaze and saw Alex walking toward them, a bunch of carrots in his hand. Her stomach tightened, but she squared her shoulders and raised her chin determinedly. *Cool, professional, distant.* She repeated the words like a mantra as he approached.

He wore white sneakers, the familiar faded jeans or another pair just like them, and an ancient Stanford football jersey, its sleeves pushed above his elbows. Only the wafer-thin gold watch on his left wrist hinted at his wealth.

He stopped beside her. "It looks like Copper King will have a double helping of carrots this afternoon."

She nodded.

"But I'm sure he won't object."

Kit extended her last carrot to the colt and said nothing.

"You're furious with me, aren't you, Kit?"

"When I walked out of the escrow office this morning, I was furious. Now I'm just resigned."

His gaze narrowed on her face. "That's wise."

She waited for Alex to finish feeding Copper King, then picked up a lead line hanging over a nail by the paddock gate, attached it to Copper King's halter, and led him from the paddock.

Alex fell into step beside her. "I'll help you with the horse." Before she could protest, he held up a restraining hand. "I know you can do it yourself, but I want to help."

And he did. They got Copper King ready for the night in less than half the usual time. Just before they closed the door of the stall, Alex turned for a last look at the colt. "Is Copper King as good as everyone seems to think he is?" he asked, running his hand over the colt's smooth cheek.

"As you know, he's timed out remarkably well," she said, frowning thoughtfully, "but I've never run him as fast as I thought he could go. He's just a baby and I didn't want to risk injuring him," she said, "but yes, he's a good one, although it's not considered proper form to say that about your own horse. I've always thought that with luck and work, he'd make a great race horse. He's got a sweet disposition, character, and heart, plus he has more raw talent than any colt I've ever seen. That's my logic talking. My instinct says he'll be the best any Randall has ever own—" She stopped. "I'm sorry. For a second I forgot he's not mine anymore."

Alex studied her with gray, mesmerizing, fiercely intelligent eyes. "I can't imagine you'd ever forget that," he said slowly. "After all, he was such a complication in your busy life. You should be delighted to be rid of him."

"I . . . am," she said quickly and, she knew, unconvincingly. She shut the door to Copper King's stall and turned away, preceding Alex out of the barn and into the long shadows of late afternoon. "Thank you for helping me with Copper King," she said, and moved toward the path to Jake's house.

Alex stopped her with a hand on her arm. "Walk with me."

She hesitated for a long moment, then told herself

that she had no choice but to do as he asked. After all, he was her employer. "All right," she said.

He led her to the lake and they stopped on its edge. When he'd established the farm, Kit's grandfather had dug the lake and planted willow trees and azaleas along its banks. It was the heart of Randall Farm, its signature. It had been so beautiful that every magazine feature or television story about the farm had included at least one picture of the lake. Now marsh grass grew along its edges and weeds threatened to engulf the few azaleas that survived. Even the willow trees looked forlorn.

Then the sun flared out in a blaze of magenta and red and gold, and the lake was beautiful again—a magical, fairytale place. She felt a simple, breath-held joy.

Alex's voice was soft, almost reverent. "I saw you just once, when you were about six. You were wearing a white dress, and standing on the island in the middle of the lake, surrounded by swans. You were laughing. I thought you were the most beautiful thing I'd ever seen." He took a step toward her, then another, and the look in his gray eyes was hypnotic. "I still do."

She pulled a leaf from a willow tree, crumbled it between thumb and forefinger, and stared down at it. "You"—she swallowed hard—". . . remember me from so long ago?"

"I couldn't forget even if I tried." He slanted her a look that took her breath away. "And I didn't want to try."

"You . . . didn't?" In spite of herself, Kit held

his gaze for several heartbeats before she glanced away. She balled her hands into fists and discovered that her palms were slick with sweat. She'd told herself that she wanted to maintain a professional relationship with Alex, but now she longed to feel his lips on hers again, to taste his mouth, to let his strong, beautiful hands rove over her heated flesh.

Something of what she was feeling must have affected Alex, too, because his voice was husky when he said, "For over twenty years I've carried that picture—you laughing, your father and mother sitting on the grass on a blue-and-white checked tablecloth with the remnants of a picnic lunch scattered around them, waving to you." Alex planted his feet and shoved his hands into the front pockets of his jeans. "That was when I realized what I wanted from life—beauty, order, a happy family, the respect of the community—all the things your father had."

Alex looked at her in a way that made her heart pound. "Until then, people thought I was headed for jail. Your father was the first person who took a chance on me, who showed me what it was like to be a real man instead of a swaggering bully.

"One of the great regrets of my life is that I didn't see him as much as I would have liked," Alex said, staring across the lake darkening to midnight blue in the waning light. "He came to San Francisco a couple of times a year and we met for lunch or dinner when I was in town."

The outside lights came on and Kit studied Alex's strong profile in their yellow glow. She wondered what it would do to him if he learned the truth about her father. Would he be so strong and hopeful and confident then? She shook her head, feeling a swift, sharp stab of hopelessness and pain. For Alex's sake, she had to keep her secret.

"You're shaking your head. What's bothering you?"

Kit scuffed her toe in the grass and a puff of dust rose. "I—I was thinking how much I have to do," she lied. "I'd better get back to Jake's."

He curled his fingers around her elbow. "There can't be that much to do. Stay a while longer."

She knew it was dangerous to be with him any longer than absolutely necessary, but the look in his eyes and the eagerness in his voice persuaded her. She nodded. "Just for a few minutes." She pulled her elbow from his grasp, and to cover her sudden confusion, she bent to pick up a stone. She settled it carefully between her thumb and forefinger, then skipped it across the smooth surface of the lake.

"Three skips," Alex said. "Not bad. My all-time record is seven, and on this very lake, if memory serves." He laughed and picked up a rock of his own. Soon they were involved in a lively contest, laughing, arguing over the best way to hold the stones and over the scoring, cheering themselves and booing each other.

Several minutes later, after a particularly good throw, Alex shouted, "I've won. You put up a good fight, but I've won! That's five skips!"

"I counted four," Kit declared, laughing. "You're

cheating!'' She cocked a fist and hit him gently on the shoulder.

He grabbed for her and she jumped back, turning to run down the path to Jake's house. Alex caught her, spun her around, and grinned down at her. He shook her playfully. ''Five!''

''Four!''

''Five!''

''You'll never persuade me. Never!''

The smile faded from Alex's face and his voice dropped very low. ''Never? Not even if I use all my powers of persuasion?''

The game was changing into something she'd vowed she'd avoid. She tried to keep her smile in place, her tone light. ''Not even then.''

Alex slid one hand to the nape of her neck and dropped the other to her waist. He moved her slowly toward him. ''Let's see about that.''

She placed her palms flat against his chest and stiffened her arms, trying to maintain the distance between them. ''Please, Alex . . .''

''I like the way your lips move when you say my name.''

Kit felt herself brought closer to him, felt the heat from his large body, smelled the fleeting, musky scent of him, stared into his hypnotic gray eyes. She was drowning, the promise she'd made to herself about keeping a professional distance tumbling about in her disordered brain.

Her arms weakened and seemingly of their own volition slid around his neck. Her breasts flattened against his chest and she turned up her lips for his kiss. His mouth was soft ... . so soft . . . and his lips rocked gently on hers, coaxing them open. He touched the tip of her tongue with his and she opened her mouth wider, welcoming him with a little cry.

The small sound seemed to inflame him and he answered with a moan, his hand tangling in her hair, his arm wrapping around her like an iron band, taking her breath. Her body trembled. She knew they should stop, but she'd never known kisses like his, had never felt the warmth that kindled inside her at his touch.

She felt tears rise behind her closed eyelids, followed by a swift surge of fear that was near panic. The tiny piece of her mind that could still think screamed a warning to stop, to run. Summoning all her willpower, she pulled her lips from his and breathed, "Alex, no," then, more strongly, "No!"

He held her away from him, his fingers tight on her upper arms. His hair was tumbled across his forehead, his breathing shallow and labored, his eyes very dark. "I want you, Kit."

Something warm and slow spiraled in her groin and she looked away from him, back toward the lake where the soft glow of the lights danced on the still, thick black water. "I . . . can't." Her voice sounded high and silly to her ears.

"All of you," he said, as if she hadn't spoken. "Your beautiful body"—he ran his hand from the flare of her hip, to her waist, to the curve of her breast—"your lovely face"—he brushed her lips with his, then touched a finger to her forehead. "And I want to know what goes on in that complicated, intelligent mind of yours. I want to know you, to share your secrets, to solve the mystery of Kit Randall.''

Her heart jerked in her chest. She was afire with wanting him. Not just *wanting*, her inner voice screamed again, *loving*! She was on the verge of loving him! But she couldn't allow him any closer. "I can't," she said again, her voice a near sob. "I just can't!"

He let her go so suddenly she almost fell. "You mean you *won't*," he said harshly, his gaze dark and furious on her face. "Maybe with one of those fancy European boyfriends, but not with me."

"That's not true! You have no idea what my life there was like."

Alex simply looked at her, the night silence stretching between them. Finally he said, "Then *tell* me what your life was like, Kit. Did a man hurt you . . . reject you? Is that what all this is about? You're determined to reject me because another man hurt you and you're afraid you'll be hurt again?"

Her anger leaped and sparked, and when she spoke her voice was breathless with it. "I hate to damage your male ego, but my refusing you has nothing to do with being rejected by a man."

"Then what *does* it have to do with?" Alex studied her, frowning, his fierce gaze probing her. Then he asked, slowly, emphasizing each word, "What were you doing those four years you spent in Europe, Kit?"

She felt a swift surge of fear that was near panic. "You forced me to stay here," she said, throwing out her arms in a gesture of anger and frustration, "but you don't own me. What I did in Europe—or anywhere else—is none of your business." Before Alex could speak again, she whirled and ran toward Jake's house as fast as her booted feet would carry her.

FIVE

Alex strode across the empty kitchen, jerked open a cabinet and extracted the bottle of twenty-year-old Scotch he'd brought along to toast his ownership of Randall Farm. He had no glasses, so he drank straight from the bottle, grimacing at the taste.

Carrying the bottle with him, he walked to the master bedroom—Oliver's old room—and threw himself onto the bed. He knew he'd have a hell of a headache in the morning, but he needed something to dull the edge of his anger and frustration. He lay in a pool of weak light from a lamp he'd placed on a packing crate beside the bed and called himself every name in the book. Then he used the words again, stringing them together in new combinations that would have made even the boys in the locker room blush.

He scowled into the gloom. He had Randall Farm,

Copper King, the best of the mares, and enough money to do anything he damned well pleased for the rest of his life. From the vibes he'd gotten at the auction and the dance, he knew plenty of women in the neighborhood were eager to share his bed.

So why wasn't he happy?

Alex clenched his jaws, making a muscle in his cheek jerk. He knew the answer to that question almost as soon as he asked it. He wanted Kit Randall and she'd rejected him. He'd always been amused by guys who went into a frenzy of frustration and despair when they were rejected by a woman. Tonight it had happened to him and he wasn't amused anymore.

Still clutching the bottle, he surged off the bed and stalked to the window. He peered through the stand of oaks at the bottom of the slope and felt a small tug of satisfaction when he saw every light on in Jake's house. Kit was sleepless, too.

Alex knew she was attracted to him. She kindled at his touch, her mouth and body hot against his lips and hands. The thought made his loins heavy and he turned away from the window to pace the room, stopping occasionally to take a pull from the bottle. He smiled humorlessly. No matter how much she denied it, Kit Randall could never forget who she was, nor that he'd been just a stablehand. He should have let her go when he had the chance. He could have hired an army of trainers, and good ones, for what he was able to pay. But he'd looked across the table at her, small and fragile and beautiful, and he'd known he had to keep her with him. When he'd threatened to cancel the sale, he'd thought she might call his bluff, and he'd experienced several seconds of sheer panic. In the end, though, she'd agreed to his demand.

That gave him six months to get her out of his system. Frowning, Alex clutched the windowsill so hard that needles of pain shot up his forearm. How the hell did a man like Oliver Randall raise a daughter who cared nothing for what he loved?

Or maybe she did care. Maybe she'd been telling the truth when she'd said the pressure of owning the farm was too much for her. Alex had already had a taste of that pressure. When word had leaked out about his pending purchase of Randall Farm, a reporter had asked to do a feature on him for *Thoroughbred Times*, and he suspected there were a lot more interview requests to come. The pressure on Kit must have been tremendous.

He sighed and raked his fingers through his already disheveled hair. "Come on, Menendez," he growled thickly. "You're making excuses for her."

He hated the way she occupied his mind. He couldn't think of the farm without thinking of her. She was attached to it, rooted in it, and he suspected that for him she always would be. "Get hold of yourself," he said contemptuously, his voice too loud in the silent room. "She's just a selfish, spoiled . . ." He let the words trail away. As a defense against his desire for Kit, he'd been clinging to that notion, but he was almost sure it wasn't true. She'd cared selflessly for Jake, she'd been devastated by his heart attack, and she'd worked hard. Her calloused hands and broken fingernails were evidence of that.

What did she have to gain by pretending otherwise?

Alex rotated the bottle and watched the brown liquid swirl up its sides. He thought of asking Jake to tell what he knew, then dismissed the idea. The loyal old man would never betray Kit's confidence—*if* he knew anything. Alex sensed there was a part of her that was hidden even from Jake.

"A mystery—that's what you are, Kit Randall," Alex said softly, his eyes narrowing. "A mystery I intend to solve."

Alex said nothing when Kit, feeling like an interloper in the house where she'd grown up, entered the huge, empty kitchen. He gestured toward the coffeepot, but she shook her head. It would have been her fourth cup on an empty stomach, and she felt nervous and slightly nauseated. Even the usually pleasant fragrance of the coffee made her stomach churn.

Alex looked terrible. Black stubble shadowed his face and dark circles had appeared under his eyes. Exhaustion had deepened the lines bracketing his mouth and thrown a gray cast over his skin. He looked haggard and completely drained, and Kit felt a swift rush of empathy. He'd spent a sleepless night, too. Then she saw the three-quarters-empty bottle of Scotch on the counter behind him and she smiled grimly. At least she wasn't hung over.

Alex followed her gaze. "I was . . . toasting my ownership of the farm."

"So I see." She swept him with her gaze, from his booted feet, black riding breeches, and gray polo shirt to his weary eyes and disheveled black hair. "It must have been quite a toast."

Alex gave a small, derisive chuckle. "It was."

"Maybe you should go back to bed."

He seared her with a long look. *Yes. With you.* If he'd carved it in stone in letters a mile high, he couldn't have conveyed his meaning more clearly.

Within her, a tight knot loosened, and desire flowed through her, insistent and hot and heavy. She blushed and looked away. He hadn't given up as she'd expected him to. She felt a dizzying mixture of relief and fear at the knowledge.

"Look at me," he said roughly, but she shook her head.

"I didn't come here to continue where we left off last night. I came to ask you what you want me to do about Copper King," she said in as cold a voice as she could manage.

"Get him ready to start at Del Mar within the month."

"He's lost some training time because of the change of ownership. That may be too soon for him," she said, her gaze on the wall, the countertop, the battered coffeepot—anywhere but at him.

"Copper King is a big, strong colt. Pushing him a little harder than you'd push an average horse won't hurt him."

"If that's what you want."

"That's what I want." He stepped closer, and against her will she raised her gaze to his. "But that's not all I want.'' His voice was steel wrapped in silk and it slid over her, caressing her skin, stroking her sensitive nerve endings, robbing her of her will to resist him.

''It's not possible. I—'' Kit's throat tightened and she couldn't finish her thought, and when he moved closer, she didn't remember what she wanted to say. He stood so close she felt the heat of his body through her thin blouse, the warmth of his breath on her cheek as he bent toward her. Then his lips crushed hers, stifling her halfhearted protest, teasing her mouth open. He raised her to her toes to bring her closer and plunged his tongue into the sweet warmth, groaning softly. She answered with a tiny whimper of desire, melting against him, weaving her fingers through his thick hair.

He became her universe, his taste in her mouth, his scent in her nostrils, and the hard strength of him pressing against her, his strong arms almost stopping her breath. He ground his hips against hers, signaling his desire, and, powerless to resist, she moved with him. A part of her mind was vaguely shocked, but her mutinous body seemed not to care.

The fragile barrier she'd built between them had cracked, and she couldn't stop it, wasn't even sure she wanted to stop it. She slid her hands down to cup his face and the stubble of his beard, as coarse as sandpaper, scratched her palms. She moved her hands down the thick column of his neck and across his broad shoulders, savoring their width and corded strength while her tongue, her lips, her lower body, performed a mating ritual as old as time.

At last he ended the kiss, but he didn't loosen his hold on Kit, which was just as well. She wasn't sure her weakened legs would hold her, especially when she looked boldly into Alex's eyes and saw the naked desire there. She'd left her hands on his shoulders and she still stood on tiptoe. "You're so . . . big," she said in a wondering voice.

"And you're so small." He slanted a heartstopping smile at her. "Small and perfect."

She ran the tip of her tongue across her lips and his gaze homed in on it. With a growl he jerked her against him again, raining kisses on her mouth, her cheeks, her hair, whispering all the shocking things he'd like to do with her when—when!—he got her into his bed.

Her heart banged against her ribs and her senses reeled. She had to stop him, to give herself time to think, to—she didn't know quite what—breathe perhaps, away from his dominating presence, his overwhelming sexuality.

"Alex, please . . ." she said, her voice soft as a warm breeze.

"Please?" Alex whispered huskily. "Please what? Kiss you again? Take you to my bed?" He moved as if to pick her up.

"Stop," she blurted, turning a deeper shade of crimson. "Please stop. Everything is moving too fast. I can't breathe . . . can't think." A shudder rippled through her. She was too vulnerable to him and he knew it. The knowledge embarrassed her profoundly.

He ran his forefinger over her lower lip, still wet

from his kisses. "This isn't about thinking, Kit. It's about feeling, about wanting . . ." He bent his head toward her, and at that instant over the pounding of blood in her ears and the loud thrumming of her heartbeat, she heard the soft toot of a horn. She'd forgotten that she and Miguel had planned to take Copper King to Lansing Farm to run sets with the other two-year-olds!

She put shaking fingers to her mouth. "I have to leave. Miguel. Copper King. . ." she said breathlessly, stupidly, gesturing with a trembling hand toward the door.

Alex stared at her for a long moment, then nodded. "I understand." He rested a hand on her shoulder, and his fingers tightened there. "But we both know this isn't over, don't we, Kit?"

She shrugged helplessly and turned away.

Alex's words still rang in Kit's ears while she waited for him and Miguel to unload Copper King from the trailer. Alex had insisted on accompanying them to the Lansings' training track, and she couldn't object. He had a right to see his colt run against other horses for the first time. He was saddling the colt himself, leaving Kit and Miguel nothing to do but stand, hands in pockets, and watch the other horses file past on their way to the track. Kit shifted nervously from foot to foot. Last night after Alex had kissed her, he'd let her run away, seeming to accept her refusal. This morning's kiss had been different. He'd appeared more determined, brushing aside her objections, his hands, his lips, his words more persuasive than ever—almost irresistible.

What did she mean almost *irresistible?* If Miguel hadn't arrived, she and Alex would have made love on the kitchen floor. She set her lips grimly and shook her head. Or anywhere else Alex chose. The thought shocked her. No one had ever had such power over her, and she was both wildly excited by the thought of making love with him and deathly afraid of it. Alex bent to check Copper King's cinch and she saw the smooth, hard curve of his buttocks. She felt her throat go dry and she looked away.

A few feet from them, Hal Davis lounged by the white board fence surrounding the track, his glittering black gaze first on the two Wentworth horses already on the track with a dozen others, then on Copper King. He rolled his ever-present cigar stub around in his mouth, offering her a glimpse of his yellowed Chiclet teeth. Then his thick lips closed again, the black stub jutting several inches in front of his broad, doughy face. If it hadn't been for Alex's winning bid, that man would be Copper King's trainer. At the thought, Kit's stomach turned over.

A red Ferrari glided to a stop beside their trailer and Marcella and Blane stepped out. "Hello, Alex," Marcella called in a low, sexy voice. She walked toward them with Blane trailing sullenly behind her. "Are you letting your new employer do all the work?" she asked, looking at Kit.

Kit had anticipated that Marcella would taunt her, but she felt a stab of pain and humiliation anyway.

She lifted her chin and looked straight into Marcella's heavily made-up green eyes. "I'm—"

"An adviser," Alex said. "Not an employee."

Kit shot him a grateful look. It was one thing to kiss her senseless when they were alone, quite another to show consideration for her feelings in front of others. She was genuinely touched by his swift defense of her.

Marcella moved closer to Alex and gazed up at him, wetting her lips. "*I'd* have been happy to . . . advise you until Jake came home from the hospital."

"I'm sure you would have," Alex said dryly, "but Kit and I have an unbreakable contract. Don't we, Kit?"

"Yes," she said weakly, instantly feeling more trapped than ever. "We . . . do."

Alex teased Kit with a sidelong glance. "Besides, where should a Randall be but at Randall Farm?"

Marcella's carefully penciled eyebrows shot skyward. "Surely you're going to change the name of the place."

Alex shook his head. "I see no reason to—unless Kit objects."

Kit's throat tightened, and to her horror, she felt as if she were about to burst into tears. She could only nod. Seconds later, she managed to stammer out, "I d-don't object." She cleared her throat. "And . . . thank you. I know my father would be pleased."

Alex was studying her, and for a moment she forgot everything but him. "And you, Kit?" he asked. "Are *you* pleased?"

"Of course."

He flashed a smile that made her weak, "I'm glad."

"Well," Marcella broke in swiftly in a too-loud voice, "how *very* lovely. Don't you think so, Blane?"

"A noble gesture," he replied sneeringly. "And the name's *much* less awkward than *Menendez Farm*."

Kit felt the awkward, hostile silence that fairly crackled between the two men and said, "I think Hal would like to talk with you, Blane." It was a blatant lie. After twenty-five years of working for the status-conscious Wentworths, Hal knew better than to intrude on their conversations, but she had to separate Alex and Blane. She didn't want angry words or blows between them, especially now, when Alex was beginning to be accepted by the community.

Kit relaxed when Blane glowered in Hal's direction, then walked stiff-backed toward him. Hal placed one fat-fingered hand on his red-and-white Wentworth Farm shirt and kneaded the great, flabby belly beneath it. He probably had an ulcer, Kit thought. His shoulders sagged humbly as Blane approached him and said something she couldn't quite hear. She recognized Blane's tone, though, and she didn't envy Hal Davis.

"Well," she said a bit too brightly, "I'd better get to work." She put on helmet and gloves, mounted Copper King, and guided the colt toward the track, nodding to Hal and Blane as she passed. Blane lifted a hand in acknowledgment, but Hal just looked at Copper King, his small eyes narrowing with hate. A sudden feeling of unease crawled from Kit's breasts to her throat and cheeks and forehead, but she fought it down. Hal hated all horses who dared to run against the Wentworth horses, even in practice. She'd lived with that knowledge almost all her life. She had no reason to worry now, she told herself firmly. But the feeling persisted, nibbling at the fringes of her mind and fluttering in her belly.

She passed a small knot of men she knew standing away from Hal and Blane, their hands shading their eyes against the slanting morning sun. They waved, but no one spoke. Today's work was important, and they seemed to feel that idle words would destroy their concentration.

The Lansings' mile-and-a-half training track was bordered by a line of cypress trees, beyond which stretched the road to Solway. On the opposite side of the track, a deep, shadowed grove of oaks rolled away toward Wentworth Farm. A duck pond surrounded by willows lay at the center of the infield of bright green, carefully tended grass. Kit heard the liquid song of a meadowlark and over it the pounding hooves and the creaking harness and the blowing of the horses' breath as they tore around the track in straining, thundering groups of four or six.

She joined another group of six for a warm-up canter. They'd go through this every morning until they headed for Del Mar, joining the others in learning the gate. By the time Copper King got to the track, the starting gate, the noise, and the other horses wouldn't spook him.

They entered a slot in the large barrier gate on wheels, waited for the others to enter, and bolted out of the slot at the sound of a loud, discordant alarm. They returned to the gate again and again, leaping from their place to the sounds of clapping and shouting and that off-key blatting. Each time Copper King shot from the gate a shade ahead of the rest and each long, leaping stride carried him farther and farther ahead of the field.

Returning to the gate for the last set, Kit glanced at the spectators, who seemed frozen in place. The trainers stared intently at the knot of horses, silently witnessing something momentous. Alex, turned away from Marcella, braced his forearms on the topmost rail of the fence, his face frozen, watching narrowly. A hundred feet or so from Alex, Blane spoke to Hal and the older man nodded, then gestured almost imperceptibly at one of the Wentworth exercise riders.

Kit's uneasy feeling persisted, but she shrugged it away again. Copper King had exceeded her expectations, running effortlessly ahead of the other horses without extending himself, unintimidated by the jostling and noise. Everything was fine. "OK, boy," she whispered, "just once more and we'll go home and get some carrots."

From the corners of her eyes she saw a flash of red in the gate to her right, another to her left. The Wentworth horses, a big bay colt and a black filly, were on either side of her this time. Kit's throat tightened and perspiration dewed her upper lip.

"You're being foolish," she muttered. "They won't try anything. They wouldn't dare."

The alarm sounded and Copper King leapt from the gate. Instantly the bay colt slammed into his side. Copper King, thrown offstride, swerved to the left, where the black filly and her rider, a swirling mass of arms and elbows and churning legs, checked him again.

This was deliberate. They were trying to injure or intimidate her colt, to make him afraid of the gate, afraid to race again. If she could fight clear, she'd simply outrun them. She gritted her teeth, dug her heels into the colt's side, and shot a gloved fist into the face of the second rider, simultaneously slamming Copper King hard against the filly's shoulder. For an instant, Kit fought her way clear, then the big bay veered into her. She lost her stirrups and frantically tried to guide Copper King with her hands and upper body. She shortened the reins, grabbed his mane, and missed. *Copper King was headed for the rail!* She shouted to him, her voice high and thin, but he didn't pause. He hit the fence with a long, shuddering "Ooof!" of pain or surprise and Kit felt herself falling. She toppled over the rail, slammed into the hard ground, and white light exploded in her head.

She slid into blackness.

Alex saw Kit fall and began to run, cursing the boots that impeded his progress. Fear and fury rose in his throat, nearly choking him. Kit had taken a real header, and he had no doubt that Wentworth was responsible. He'd pay for this, but right now Alex had to get to Kit.

Sweating, breathing hard, terror twisting in his gut, he reached the knot of men and horses gathered on the track side of the rail. He vaulted over it, elbowed his way through the smaller group of men gathered around Kit, and knelt beside her. "Kit!" he said in a strangled voice. "Kit!"

Someone had removed her helmet and he touched the spill of bright hair, ran his forefinger down her white face to wipe away a trickle of blood running from her hairline to her chin. He picked up her hand, every prayer he knew running through his head. Her skin was cool and God knew what kind of head injuries she'd sustained. "Call an ambulance," he ordered in a shaking, husky voice he'd never heard before.

Miguel's voice came out of the group of men. "I've already sent one of the boys to do that, boss."

Alex put his cheek close to her face and felt the faint warmth of her breath. A tiny sound, more sigh than moan, came from her lips. Far too slowly, her eyelids fluttered open and she stared at him as if she didn't know him.

"Kit!" he said desperately.

"Copper . . . King."

Alex had forgotten the colt. He looked questioningly around the circle of men.

A skinny Hispanic kid with a tentative beard was holding Copper King. "He looks like he's OK, Mr. Menendez," the boy said. "I think he's just scared."

Kit struggled to sit up. "I want to see him, to make sure—"

"He's fine. You can see him later," Alex said soothingly. One of the trainers handed him a wet towel and he began to wipe the blood and dirt from Kit's face.

An eternity later, he heard the wail of a siren in the distance.

Alex slammed on the brakes and the Mercedes skidded to a stop in front of the huge, white-columned Wentworth mansion. He leapt from the cab, pounded up the steps to the front door, and punched the door- bell. He tapped his booted foot impatiently until the door opened and a perfect, formally dressed butler peered at him. "I'd like to see Mr. Wentworth," Alex said in a voice that conveyed he was in no mood to tolerate a refusal.

"Mr. Wentworth is on the terrace," the butler said, pointing to the rear of the house.

"No need to announce me, then. I'll find him my- self." Ignoring the butler's startled look, Alex took the front steps two at a time, vaulted a hedge, and loped toward the terrace.

Blane sat in a chair drawn up to a glass-topped table, a drink in front of him, a copy of *The Racing Gazette* in one slim-fingered hand. Marcella, bikinied and oiled, her voluptuous body turned toward the sun, reclined on a chaise longue. She sat up as Alex approached, began to smile, then stopped when she saw his expression. "We're *so* sorry about Kit," she said. "How *is* she?"

"She'll be fine." Alex strode toward Blane and jerked him to his feet, one large hand clutching Blane's shirtfront, the other coiling into a fist. "No thanks to you."

Blane's too-blue eyes widened with fear. "I . . had . . . nothing to do with what happened to Kit."

"You know damned well that your riders went after her and the colt. You knew they couldn't outrun Copper King, so you decided to intimidate him—to scare him so he'd quit." He gave Blane a shake. "But that colt has heart and brains. It'll take more than a roughing up to make a quitter of him. And as for what you did to Kit—"

Blane's well-shaped lips drew back from his perfect teeth in a snarl, and he wasn't handsome anymore. "Racing's a tough, dangerous game. Kit knew the chance she was taking."

"She didn't know anybody would be low enough to deliberately hurt her."

"You have no proof I hurt her, Menendez! Now let me go!"

"I have all the proof I need." Alex released Blane, calculated the distance between them, and smashed his fist against Blane's perfect nose. Blane fell back against the table, the glass shattered, and a shower of bright shards rained around him.

Blane lay cursing and crying, blood streaming from between his fingers. "Damn you, Menendez," he screamed. "I'll get you for this!" He began to flop around like a gaffed fish, the glass crunching under him, blood staining his shirtfront. "Don't just stand there, Marcella. Help me up!"

She stood and stuck out a bare foot. "You wouldn't want me to cut my feet, would you, brother dear?" She looked at the butler, who had appeared in the doorway. "Help Mr. Wentworth, please, Harrison." A smile curved her mouth. "He seems to have run into Mr. Menendez's fist."

Harrison, his long, straight nose wrinkling slightly, picked his way through the glass and held out a perfectly manicured hand. "Sir."

Clutching Harrison's hand, Blane struggled to his feet. "You haven't heard the end of this. I'll tell everyone and you'll be finished here, you—" Blane's screams ended in a gurgle.

"Get out the car, Harrison. Mr. Wentworth needs a doctor," Marcella said as the two men moved toward the house, Blane leaning heavily on the butler. She placed a hand on Alex's forearm. "You're some kind of man, Alex Menendez," she said, her voice very low.

Alex looked coldly down at her. "You like the sight of blood, don't you, Marcella?" he asked. "I'd have thought you'd show a little compassion for your brother."

Her voluptuous lips thinned and her magnificent shoulders lifted in a shrug. "My brother is a fool." She wet her lips. "But you, Alex Menendez, definitely are not."

"That's why I want no part of the Wentworths— *either* of them."

Hectic red spots appeared high on Marcella's cheeks and her uncanny green eyes burned like live embers. "It's Kit, isn't it? You're in love with Kit Randall!" Marcella laughed a hard, angry laugh.

Alex started. "Hardly." He wanted Kit, all right, passionately, single-mindedly, but as for loving her . . . He frowned and looked down at Marcella without seeing her. Instead, he saw Kit's golden hair, her deep-blue eyes. His loins grew heavy with desire. That was all it was, he told himself. Plain, old-fashioned lust. The sooner he got Kit Randall out of his system, the better.

He drove like a maniac back to Randall Farm.

─────────── SIX ───────────

Kit lay propped on pillows on the sofa in Jake's small living room, a light blanket drawn up under her arms. The blanket wasn't for warmth—the heat was stifling— but to protect her pajama-clad body from Alex's assessing gaze. She twisted around to stare at him, her eyes wide with surprise. Then they flashed angrily when she began to understand exactly what he'd said, and the implications of his statement. "You hit Blane?" she asked, her voice rising. "You actually *hit* him?"

"I broke his nose," Alex replied matter-of-factly.

"I don't believe this!" She bit her lip, counted silently to ten, and went on in a voice she managed to make a little less hysterical. "I took you to the dance and introduced you to the neighbors, most of whom seemed to like you. I worked hard to get you accepted, and I thought you would be. Instead, you beat up one of them."

Alex glowered at her. "I did what I thought was appropriate."

"You call that *appropriate*? You flattened the man's nose!" Kit's head hurt and the cut just above her hairline stung. She felt stiff and sore in places she'd never been aware of before. She wanted quiet and solitude, and instead she had this impossibly stubborn man to contend with—a man who thought it was "appropriate" to beat a neighbor—or part of a neighbor—to a pulp. For an instant a tiny, perverse piece of her mind longed to have witnessed the scene on the Wentworth terrace. She managed to keep her disapproving look firmly in place, though, and Alex looked back at her just as grimly.

"What you've said doesn't change anything. I'd hit Wentworth again."

"I'll just bet you would. You'll never learn, will you?"

"I'll never learn to stand quietly by and let some clown issue orders to brutalize my horse and his rider." Alex raked his hand through the silky thickness of his hair. "My God, Kit, you and the colt could have been killed! Doesn't that mean anything to you?"

"Of course it means something! But there were ways of handling this—acceptable ways. You could have gone to Charles and asked him to investigate through the breeders' organization—"

"And Wentworth would get his aristocratic hand slapped by the other members of your crowd and he'd go back to being the arrogant bastard he's always been."

"He'll be that anyway," she said quietly, trying to restrain her fury, to inject the sound of sweet reason into her voice. "Don't you see that if you'd asked Charles to investigate the incident you'd have had the support of the community? But you've handled things so barbarically I don't know how they'll feel."

Alex reeled back as though she'd slapped him, and a flush of red washed along his jawline. "I was a gutter kid—a street fighter. I learned to hit out hard and fast. If that makes me a barbarian to people like you, then so be it. I don't give a damn."

Her anger rose again, red and hot. "I didn't say you were a barbarian. *I said you handled the situation in a barbaric way,* and that if you keep acting like that you'll never fit in here."

Alex snapped out a curse. "Fitting in with your country club friends isn't important to me."

"It should be," she practically shouted. "If it were just a matter of country club dances and cocktail parties, you'd be right not to care, but many of the people around here are damned good horse breeders. You need their knowledge and experience. Someday you may even need *them.* Jake or I won't always be here to advise you, you know."

"I don't need anybody." A shadow of sadness passed across Alex's face, then his expression hardened and he squared his shoulders, drew his lips tightly together. "Not anymore."

He was thinking of her father. Kit knew that as surely as if Alex had spoken his thoughts aloud. She thought of the confused, angry, needy boy he must have been when he met her father, but she pushed the thought away. She wasn't going to allow herself to feel sorry for what she'd said. She was angry and, dammit, she was going to *stay* angry. "Then what am *I* doing here?" She sat up quickly, her aching body moaning a protest at the suddenness of her movement. "If you don't need me to manage the farm, let me go. You're taking six months from my life when I could be—"

"Getting a suntan?"

Kit didn't know which made her angrier—Alex's words or the sneer that accompanied them. "Let me go, Alex," she repeated in a voice husky with rage and frustration.

"Not a chance."

"You're just keeping me here to"—Kit's throat tightened as a hot flush rushed over her from the soles of her feet to the roots of her hair—"amuse yourself."

Alex was still for the space of a heartbeat. Then he rapped out, "That's not true. I don't play with people."

He'd hesitated a fraction too long and his tone was a bit too defensive. Kit didn't believe him. "I think you do. Or you run over them, as you did with Blane."

"You keep coming back to Wentworth. People of your class stick together, don't they, Kit?" Alex asked in a soft, deadly voice. "It must kill you to work for a barbarian like me."

She waved aside his accusation. She'd defended herself against it once too often, and she was in no mood to argue about it again. She sighed wearily and said, "Let me leave here as soon as Jake is well. You can hire someone else to manage the farm. Let me get on with my life."

"A life of suntans and parties and . . ." He lifted his voice suggestively on the last word.

Her anger, simmering just under her barely controlled surface, surged again. "You know nothing about my life, but you attack my morals as if you did," she gritted out through clenched teeth. "Who the devil do you think you are?"

"The man you have an unbreakable contract with—a contract you publicly acknowledged just this morning. I'm also the guy who thinks you have a responsibility to help fix the place you ruined."

"Is that why you're keeping me here? To punish me?" Kit stared up at him in mute fury. A strange expression lurked in his clear gray eyes and pulled at the corners of his mouth. He was lying again, or at least not telling the whole truth. "You thought I was too lazy to run the farm when I owned it. What makes you think I'll do the job now?"

"Because I know you're not lazy no matter what you pretend. You work as hard as anybody I've ever known. I don't want you to ride Copper King again, though. I'll hire an exercise rider."

"But I *want* to ride him," she protested. Realizing her longing was reflected in her eyes and voice, she made her face blank, but she was too late. Alex had noticed.

"That's obvious." His searching gaze measured

her. "When you came to, your first thought was of him. You love the horse, don't you, Kit?"

"I told you that."

"You told me *he* liked *you*, that you could handle him when no one else could, but that the colt was a complication you wanted to get rid of."

"There's nothing contradictory about that." Kit didn't meet Alex's gaze. "I love Copper King, but I don't—*didn't*—have a place for him in my life, so I sold him."

"Why do I think you're telling me the truth, but not the whole truth?"

And why do I feel the same way about you? She looked out the window, where the first haze of twilight purpled the sky. "I don't know what you mean." She stiffened defensively when Alex sat beside her on the couch, drew a lock of hair from the gleaming mass falling over her shoulder, and began rolling it around his forefinger.

He gave her a lazy, predatory smile. "I think you know exactly what I mean."

She should order him out of the house, or run upstairs and lock the door behind her. But, impaled by his relentless gray gaze, she couldn't speak or move or breathe. She didn't even feel the aches and pains from her fall anymore. She seemed to float, weightless, just looking at him.

He'd seemed so terrified when he'd helped to load her into the ambulance this morning, so tender when he'd carried her into the house after her release from the hospital. And his fury with Blane, while she didn't condone what Alex had done, was understandable.

"You do know what I mean, don't you, Kit?" he prodded.

She wet her lips. "Please . . . let's not talk about that."

"Then what shall we talk about? You . . . and me? When you fell this morning, I thought you'd been badly hurt or killed and I was terrified."

She couldn't breathe, couldn't look away, and her heart constricted like a suddenly caged bird. The air seemed warmer and thicker. A faint dew of moisture beaded her skin.

A sexual current so strong it robbed her of breath throbbed in the room and in the darkening, empty house that lay beyond it. She felt several seconds of sheer panic, then threw back her head to pull the lock of hair from his grasp. She raised her head a stubborn fraction of an inch and took a deep breath. All she had to do was keep her wits about her and stay calm.

"I'd like . . . to rest now," she said in a voice that trembled with barely suppressed desire.

His mesmerizing gray eyes were unwavering, gleaming silver in the fading light. "You've been resting for the better part of the day. You're not tired, you're scared."

She felt a short, sharp tug of indignation at his words. "What could I possibly be scared of?" She silently cursed the quaver in her voice.

"Me." He tangled his fingers in the soft fall of her hair, cupped the curve of her skull. He held her in place while his lips brushed hers once, then again. He moved back from her, his eyelids drooping as if suddenly heavy. "I don't know all I want to about you, but I know that."

She tried for a calm voice while her heart thudded in her throat so hard he must see the pulse beating there. "Why should I be afraid of you?"

"Because you want me, and that's a threat to your beloved independence—and to your pride."

Embarrassment and anger warred in her and she chose the anger, gathering it around her like a shield. "I don't want you," she snapped, and knew as she said it that he wouldn't believe her. How could he, when she herself didn't believe her words?

"Yes, you do, and I'm about to prove it." He jerked the thin blanket away from her and dropped it to the floor. Before she could move away from him, he pulled her against him, taking her mouth in an angry kiss, sweet and hot, that robbed her of the last shred of the power she'd thought she possessed.

His tongue assaulted her lips, demanding entrance. A hurricane raged inside her. He wanted her and she, him.

Oh, how she wanted him.

With a tiny moan, a mixture of defeat and desire, she gave way to him, opening her mouth to welcome him, to taste him.

He kissed her harder, made throaty, urgent sounds, and pressed her back against the pillows, his body heavy on hers. He became her world, his lips against hers, his voice in her ears, his scent in her nostrils. She arched against him, a bundle of quivering nerves and fevered longings. She tangled her fingers in the silky thickness of his hair to draw him closer and he deepened the kiss, his tongue thrusting in and out, in and out, maddening her with each deliberate stroke and signaling his intentions more clearly than words ever could.

She felt his arousal against her hip and pressed against it, her desire making her bold. Growling, he thrust two fingers under the waistband of her pajamas and stripped them off, tossing them in the direction the blanket had gone.

His hands moved possessively over the naked skin of her thighs and buttocks and the soft flesh of her waist. He cupped her breasts under the thin fabric of her pajama tops, then, his hands shaking but lightning swift, he tore away the buttons and slid the fabric down over her arms, freeing her from the confinement of her clothing, leaving her naked before him.

He parted her thighs and booted, still clothed, knelt between them, raking her from head to toe with eyes that were glazed and wild. "I knew you'd be beautiful, but my Lord . . ." His hands followed the path of his gaze, and her passion swelled and built. She reached out to pull him down to her, but with a muffled oath, he levered himself off the couch. She had only the briefest glimpse of his dark muscular body as he stripped off his clothes and then he was beside her again, rising over her, raising her hips to meet him.

She welcomed him into the warm, soft core of her with a cry, and their joining was fast, angry, frantic.

She couldn't get enough of him, nor he of her. The intensity was so great she knew it couldn't last, and the explosion, when it came, shook her with the force of an earthquake. She lay weak and shaking in its aftermath, her heart beating so hard it hurt.

He rolled onto his side, taking her with him, and for long minutes they lay, still joined, pressed together in the narrow space, their eyes closed, their bodies sheened with sweat, their breathing slowly returning to normal.

Kit felt the lift of Alex's weight, then a slight shift of air, and he was gone. He retrieved the blanket and placed it over her.

She lifted a still-trembling hand to push back a lock of damp hair that had fallen across her eyes and, wordless, her heart catching in her throat, watched him dress.

He was magnificent. Broad-shouldered, narrow-waisted, lean-hipped, he moved smoothly to pick up his boots and jeans. He slanted a look at her and she closed her eyes, embarrassed to be caught gazing at him. She felt rather than saw his smile.

When she looked at him again he was facing her, his shirt dangling from his fingers. "I intended for that to happen, but not the way it did. I'd hoped our first time would be more . . . romantic."

"Our first time!" she blurted out indignantly, and sat up. The blanket fell away and his heated gaze seared her before she clutched it to her again. "You certainly take a lot for granted."

"I know we're attracted to one another." He moved toward her. "Irresistibly attracted. To pretend you can fight it is a waste of time and emotional energy.'' He wove his fingers into her hair. ''Energy that's better spent on making love.''

''That's not—''

He jerked her to her knees and caught her words with his open mouth, kissing her senseless, robbing her of breath and speech. The blanket fell away again and she caught her breath as her breasts rubbed against the soft hair of his chest. Too soon, he ended the kiss and moved away from the sofa, still watching her.

A fresh wave of warmth washed her body when she realized how foolish she must look, kneeling on the sofa, the blanket forgotten, still reaching out to him.

''You see?'' he asked huskily and grinned his quick white grin.

Anger flared in her again, hot and pricking. She covered herself and glowered at him.

His smile faded. ''You hate it that you're attracted to me and that I know it. That gives me power over you, and you can't stand that, can you, Kit?'' He touched her cheek.

She jerked her head away. ''What I think and feel is none of your business.''

''I'm making it my business. I've already told you that I want to know all about you.''

Her gaze flew to his, widened. Fear began to crawl in her stomach. ''Leave me alone, Alex,'' she said softly.

He simply stood where he was, searching her face for a sign of softening, but she couldn't relent. Her family's reputation and her father's good name depended on her silence.

So did Alex's happiness.

Her heart leapt, seemed to still for a moment as she realized her priorities had shifted. Alex's happiness had become more important to her than the Randall name.

She was in love with him!

But he was only amusing himself with her.

She knew she'd gone slack-faced with shock and that Alex was watching her narrowly, trying to read her thoughts. "This can't happen again," she said in a strangled voice. "We've got to forget it ever happened at all."

"Not forget," he said. "I can't, and neither can you."

"We have to go back to the way we were."

"The way we were *when*? Last night, when I kissed you? Or this morning when I kissed you again? Or the night of the dance"—he grinned—"when you kissed me? Face it, Kit, our lovemaking is becoming a habit—one I don't care to break."

"If you don't break it, I'll leave."

He stilled, looking at her levelly. "Our contract—"

"Our contract be damned. You'll have to sue me—*if* you can find me."

"You'd run away?"

She nodded. "If I have to."

He ran his fingers through his hair and Kit could almost feel its silky thickness between her fingers. "You won't have to," he said, and sighed. "I'll agree to do what you want."

But it isn't what I want! It's what I have to do!
She nodded, but didn't speak. She knew she couldn't
trust her voice.

The groan and snarl of heavy equipment and the
sound of hammers and power saws nearly drowned
out Jake's words, and Kit had to sit forward on the
shabby old couch to hear him. Even though his voice
was still weak, color had returned to his cheeks and
his eyes sparkled with excitement. "That Alex sure
get things done," he said delightedly. "I can't wait
to get out there and see the new barn."

"You take it easy," Kit cautioned. "You've been
home just a few hours. The barn will keep." Seeing
Jake's disappointment, she added, "Alex is really
going all out on it, though. There'll be a foaling
stall, washing stalls, a small vet hospital, housing for
the grooms, and stabling for twenty horses. Eventu-
ally, there will be a swimming pool for the horses
in that little glade south of the barns."

She set her lips and fought back the envy that rose
in her every time she thought of the improvements
Alex was making. "It's everything I ever dreamed
of," she admitted. "Once construction is finished,
he's going to move in the horses and start immedi-
ately on the other barn."

Jake smiled admiringly, his pale old eyes alight.
"That Alex . . ."

And she'd been worried that Jake wouldn't adjust
to Alex's ownership! Instead, Alex had become a
hero to the old man. She stifled a sigh and looked
out the window to where a bulldozer was recountour-

ing the shores of the lake. "Remember the pink and white azaleas that used to grow there?"

"Red ones, too, if I remember right."

"I'll send Alex a memo about them."

"Maybe they'd get replanted faster if you'd just tell him." Jake lifted his thin white eyebrows. "I think things go better when people talk to each other, don't you?"

"Alex and I have nothing to say to each other."

Jake snorted disgustedly. "I sure can't figure out why you took up for that Blane Wentworth. He's needed a licking since he was knee high, and I'm dead certain that a lot of people are cheering because Alex finally went and did it."

Kit felt her temper rising and controlled it with an effort. "There are better ways to resolve differences than by fighting about them."

"Alex was defending you and Copper King. I sure can't fault him for that. And I can't fault him for hitting Hal Davis, either." Jake chuckled. "Years ago I heard one of the Wentworth stablehands had knocked Hal silly. I just didn't know it was Alex." Kit had never seen Jake look more pleased.

She shook her head disgustedly.

"Alex said your daddy knew about it and gave him a job anyway. That didn't surprise me any. I told him Oliver helped out a lot of people."

Kit leaned forward, suddenly tense. "Did you tell him . . . anything else?"

"You mean about your daddy having money trouble there toward the end?" To Kit's relief, Jake shook his head. "That's Randall business and I'd never let anybody in on it. It sort of hurts that you think I would.''

Stung, Kit placed her hand on his. ''Oh, Jake, I'm sorry!''

''It's all right,'' he said soothingly, patting her hand. ''I know you aren't yourself lately.''

She jerked upright, her eyes widening. ''What gave you that idea?''

''It's clear to anybody who'd take the time to look that you're feeling poorly. You love this place and you had to sell it. Anybody would take on about that.'' He nodded, watching her closely. ''And now you're feuding with Alex.''

''I wouldn't call it feuding—exactly.''

''It's natural that you'd resent him, Kit. He bought the farm and you wanted to keep it, and—''

''You didn't tell him that!''

''There you go again,'' Jake said, sighing. ''Course I didn't. We talked about the horses, and your daddy, and Consuelo, the woman who raised him. He calls her his aunt, but she's no blood relation. He's real fond of her and her two kids, though. He sent both of them to college, just like your daddy did for him.''

She knew Jake would have been happy to gossip for hours about Alex, but she decided not to ask anything more. If she did, she risked sending Jake's matchmaking instincts into overdrive. ''Alex is a very generous man,'' she said in a tone that tried to convey that the subject of Alex was, for a while at least, closed. ''How about lunch? I've made cucumber soup, and it won't take a minute to fix a salad to go with it.''

"You've been working hard, Kit. You need more than that. Steak and cottage fries, that's the ticket."

"Soup and salad for both of us," she insisted stubbornly, heading for the kitchen. The man was mad about red meat and cholesterol, but he wouldn't get them from her. She wanted him around for a long, long time.

She'd almost finished putting the lunch on a tray when the bulldozer operator cut the engine of his huge, noisy machine. Relieved by the sudden silence, she sighed, then drew in her breath, suddenly tense when she heard the low rumble of Alex's voice coming from the living room.

She had to face him. The thought jolted her, set her hands trembling so much she dropped a spoon, wincing as it clattered to the floor. She tucked in her shirttail, smoothed her hair, and counted to ten to slow the rapid flutter of her heart.

She hadn't seen Alex in the two weeks since they'd made love. He'd kept in touch with his construction foreman by telephone from the Summit Enterprises office in San Francisco, and with her by means of a blizzard of memos demanding answers to the minutest questions about the farm and horses. Nothing he'd asked could faintly be construed as personal.

She'd alternated between relief and a deep disappointment that kept her sleepless through the long, hot nights. By day she'd worked like a demon, trying to keep her thoughts away from Alex, assuring herself that he hadn't been serious, that he'd only been amusing himself at her expense and keeping her at the farm to punish her.

She picked up the tray and headed for the living room, moving like a puppet, heavy and numb. She paused a moment in the dark, shabby hallway to compose herself before she stepped into the room. "Hello, Alex," she said in a much softer and warmer voice than she'd intended. Alex sat on the sofa in the place she'd vacated—the one closest to Jake—and the two of them had their heads together like conspirators.

Alex stood and reached for the tray. "Let me help you with that."

"I can manage," she said reflexively, drawing back when his fingers grazed hers, her face flushing.

"Humor me. Let me feel useful." He put the tray on the coffee table and carefully served the old man's lunch.

"Would you like something to eat, Alex?" Kit asked, feeling awkward and foolish, drawn to him as strongly as ever, but perversely wanting him far away so that she wouldn't feel so on edge, so fearful she'd betray her continuing attraction to him with a look or a gesture.

"No, thanks." He jerked off his tie, folded it neatly, and put it into the pocket of his blue sports jacket, which lay across the back of the sofa. He settled onto the couch again, perfectly at home.

As she ate, she watched him through the thick screen of her lashes. He looked tired, his face thinner, dark smudges under his eyes. He placed his palm behind his neck and rotated his head, trying to ease the stiffness there. She wanted to go to him and rub his pain away.

She jerked bolt upright. She had to stop thinking like this, dreaming of touching him, dreaming of . . .

Jake studied her intently, a smug smile playing around his lips. "What's the matter, Kit?" he asked. "Why, you're downright pale."

"N-nothing. I feel . . . fine." She ate her meal more rapidly than good manners dictated, stood, and began to clatter her dishes back onto the tray.

Alex waved her back to her chair. "That can wait. I have something to show you." He picked up a cardboard tube that lay on the floor, opened one end, removed a roll of blueprints, and spread them on the table.

Jake leaned forward. "That's a real pretty house, Alex."

"I'm glad you like it. It's designed by the same architect who's going to remodel the main house."

Except for Jake's house, all the buildings at Randall Farm were designed in the Spanish-mission style, and this one matched the rest, with a wide front porch running the length of its long, low facade, graceful floor-to-ceiling arched windows, and tiled roof. Inside was a large living room-dining room combination, a good-sized kitchen, and two master suites, one at each end of the house. "It's beautiful," Kit said. "Are you going to use it as a guest house?"

Alex hesitated, and an expression she hadn't seen before crossed his face. For a moment, she glimpsed a small boy, eager but uncertain. "It's your house if you want it, Jake."

Slack-jawed, Jake stared at him. "Mine?"

"It has large rooms and they're all on one level. That makes it easier for you to get around. The two big bedrooms separated from each other will give you privacy and room enough for a live-in house-keeper if you ever need one."

Jake looked doubtful. "It'll cost an awful lot."

"That's my worry."

Jake glanced around the small, shabby room. "Evvie and I had some real good times in this old house." The grooves around his thin mouth deepened. "What do you think, Kit?"

"I think . . ." Her throat tightened and her eyes misted. "I think it's perfect."

Jake's gaze returned to the blueprints and he nodded emphatically. "It sure is."

"Then you'll accept it?" Alex prodded.

The old man's eyes were pink with tears. "I'll accept it, and thank you. Nobody's ever given me a present like this. Nobody."

Kit gazed at Alex and knew that everything she felt for him showed in her eyes. He'd offered Jake a comfortable home and a secure future. Without meaning to, probably without giving it a second thought, Alex had freed her from her worries about the old man.

Alex's eyes held hers, very gray. He didn't smile. She didn't look away. She felt her joints soften like tallow held to flame. Her heart began a slow, dragging, hammering beat. Her mouth went dry. The room was so silent he must hear her heart. "Thank you," she said, and thrust herself from her chair. Almost before she knew she was doing it, she was running up the stairs to her tiny room.

SEVEN

Kit rose before dawn, dressed hurriedly in jeans, boots, and an old blue polo shirt and tiptoed down the stairs, careful not to awaken Jake. She'd hoped he'd sleep for several more hours. He certainly needed the rest. Alex had left a copy of the blueprints for the new house with him, and in spite of her efforts to get him to sleep, Jake had spent the day and a large part of the night poring over them.

She stepped into the silvery, predawn light and drew in a long, quavering breath of still-cool air. It carried with it the wonderful bouquet of oak and freshly turned earth and newly cut grass. In the distance one of the mares whinnied and Kit sensed rather than heard the faint flurry of movement from the barn. She loved the farm at dawn, loved the first tiny stirrings of men and animals as they began their day.

This dawn carried with it a special sharpness, a singing, vibrating intensity she'd felt few times in her life. She planned to have Ben Wolfhunter, the exercise rider Alex had hired, run Copper King all out for the first time, and the adrenaline that rushed through her made her hearing more acute, smells and sounds and colors sharper.

She emerged from the trees and the racetrack lay before her. Alex's men had plowed the mile-and-a-half oval, and rich black loam lay soft and sweet-smelling across its width. They'd painted the brown four-board fence that surrounded it, and replaced the old starting gate with a state-of-the-art gate of the kind found only at the best racetracks. Kit knew she'd be shocked by the price tag.

Envy pricked at her. *You should be happy the farm will be beautiful again,* she admonished herself, *even if you won't be here to enjoy it.* A long, slow shudder wracked her body at the thought of leaving the place, and she waited for it to pass, then thrust the thought aside. Copper King's workout was all that was important today, and she had to concentrate on that.

She turned when she heard the slow drag of Copper King's hooves on the loam and saw Alex and Miguel leading the colt. The rest of the grooms and Ben clustered around the horse. Everyone seemed to be touching Copper King for luck or whispering encouragement and promising him extra carrots if he did well.

"Where's Jake?" Alex asked when they stopped near her.

"Still sleeping, I hope. I thought the excitement might be too much for him."

"He'll be furious."

"I know, but I'll have to risk it." The colt looked wonderful—alert and gleaming, the dappling on his rump indicating his perfect condition. Kit yearned to ride him. She cast an oblique, envious glance at Ben, then asked Miguel, "How does the colt seem to you?"

"Fit and ready."

"Seems that way to me, too," Ben added. He was a Sioux, a tiny brown leaf of a man with a good seat, strong hands, and a calm air. He whispered to the colt in his musical language and Copper King pricked his ears, listening. "You're going to do great this morning, aren't you, big fella?" Ben winked. "The colt says he'll fly."

They laughed nervously as Ben mounted the colt, clucked softly, and headed him toward the track. "I'd settle for a good, fast work with all four of his feet on the ground at the end," Kit called, and they all laughed again. They clustered near the fence, a silent group of eight—Kit, Alex, Miguel, and the five other grooms—their forearms propped on the fence, their bodies angled forward and tight with tension.

"Having Ben ride the colt is for the best, Kit," Alex said too softly for the others to hear. He'd seen her look at Ben and read her thoughts. "You're the boss," she said flatly as the horse and rider began their warm-up canter. "I just follow orders."

She felt Alex's eyes on her, knew he wanted to

say something more, and sensed exactly when he thought better of it and followed her gaze. She pulled a stopwatch from her pocket and thumbed it nervously. "Six furlongs—three-quarters of a mile—that's as far as you have to go," she muttered. "It's just a sprint."

"Talking to yourself?" Alex asked.

"To Copper King."

"He can't hear you. Do you think you two have some sort of psychic connection?"

"Sometimes."

Alex looked at her curiously, but said nothing.

Copper King stepped calmly into the starting gate. Good. He was using no more of his energy—physical or emotional—than he had to. Kit's heartbeat doubled. She bit her lip, heard the loud, discordant sound that signaled the opening of the gate, and punched her thumb down on the watch.

The colt bolted forward and surged along, his tearing, thundering strides lengthening and quickening. As he approached the tiny knot of silent watchers, she heard the jingle and squeak of his harness, the whalelike blowing of his breath, the soft urging of Ben's voice. They were magnificent—man and horse a single unit, the big red colt moving with powerful, flowing grace, his tiny rider, arms outstretched, close to the colt's neck. Kit needed no stopwatch to know they were flying, as Ben had promised.

She punched the watch when Copper King flashed under the wire, then stared down at it, openmouthed, unable for an instant to believe what she saw. *He's done it, Daddy. Just as you knew he would.*

Seven pairs of eyes stared at her. "Well?" Alex prodded.

"One minute, seven seconds," she managed to say.

The grooms whooped wildly and began to dance, laughing and chanting the time, shouting it to Ben, who raised a victorious fist and grinned.

"Obviously that's good," Alex said, "but *how* good?"

"It's one . . . one-fifth of a second off the world's record for six furlongs," she said in a small, still-disbelieving voice.

Alex stood very still absorbing the information. Then he asked, "OK, so what do we do now?"

"We do slow works all week so that the colt can stay sharp and get back some energy and then we run him all out to make sure today's time wasn't a fluke."

"And if it wasn't?"

The grooms were listening now, their eyes on her. Behind them, Ben had slowed the colt to a canter. Copper King moved alertly, head up, only the faintest wash of sweat visible on his neck and shoulders. He'd come through the workout wonderfully.

"If he does well the next time, there's a race at Del Mar at the end of the month I'd like to enter him in."

Miguel shook his head doubtfully. "I hear the Wentworths have entered Nightwatch in that race."

Kit lifted her chin and glared a challenge at him. "Are we going to let a Wentworth horse scare us off?"

"He's real good," Miguel said, "and he already has three wins under his belt. The last was a stakes race."

"If our colt does well again, I'm going to take the chance," she said stubbornly.

Alex had been looking first at Kit, then at Miguel. Now his gaze swung back to Kit. "*What* chance? What race are you talking about?" he demanded.

"The Commencement Stakes," Kit said, and clutched the stopwatch like a talisman.

After Copper King made his near world-record run, an air of excitement pervaded the farm, and when he ran just as fast a week later, the sense of expectation became almost palpable. Even the plumbers and carpenters working on the barn and the bulldozer operators grading the roads seemed to catch the fever. Every morning before work they lined the fence to watch Copper King run. Alex reveled in the excitement. Only once before, during the summer when Black Moon Rising had won the Triple Crown, had he felt anything so wonderful, so addictive. The calls that came from Summit Enterprises increasingly irritated him, and he counted the days until the new owners would take over the business and leave him free to devote all his attention to the farm. He'd already sold his San Francisco penthouse.

Standing under the huge oak at the bottom of the lawn, he sipped his morning coffee and looked across the farm's sprawling width. At first, he'd dreamed of keeping the place as a tribute to Oliver, but now he loved it with a passionate intensity he'd never felt before.

Randall Farm was all he'd ever need.

Kit's clear, trilling laughter made him raise his head. She and Miguel were leading one of the mares toward the paddock, and at the sight of her, Alex reacted as he always did—with a swift tightening of his gut and an uncontrollable quickening of his heartrate.

Damn, but the woman frustrated him! He wanted to follow her, to pull her onto the soft grass in the shade of a tree and make love to her again—not quickly this time, but slowly, gently, until they were both satiated, languid with lovemaking.

He remembered how she'd felt under him, now lush and full her breasts had been. Her skin was satin, her hair golden silk, and she'd smelled of wildflowers, sage, and summer air. Kit had been as passionate as he, as urgent as he, and she'd shaken him to his toes—surprising him, stimulating him, and satisfying him. *Almost* satisfying him, he amended quickly. He still didn't know her. The wise man who'd said the way to get to know a woman was by taking her to bed hadn't met Kit Randall.

Frowning, Alex fought the flood of desire that threatened to engulf him. Strange that he'd thought of what they'd done as "making love." He'd never thought of sex that way before. And Marcella had accused him of being in love with Kit. He'd denied it, of course. What he felt for Kit was lust, simple and straightforward.

He sipped his coffee again, found it cold, and

dumped it on the ground. It was lousy anyway. He hadn't had a decent cup of coffee since the last morning he'd spent with his aunt in San Francisco. Damn, but he missed Consuelo. She'd have been here by now if she hadn't had so many friends to say goodbye to. She was a simple woman with an enormous gift for friendship, and she read people as easily as he read a financial report. He smiled humorlessly at the thought. If anyone could help him figure Kit out, it would be Consuelo.

Kit was calling to one of the grooms. She and Miguel had released the mare into the paddock and were walking back to the barn. The sunlight glinted on her golden hair and her hips swayed provocatively in her tight, faded jeans. Alex swore softly. He hated confusion, hated the turmoil of emotions he felt every time he looked at Kit. He liked order, peace, a predictable routine, the single-minded pursuit of a goal, whether it was a college degree or business success or buying and improving Randall Farm. No woman had ever muddled his thoughts as Kit had.

Hell, he was a classic case of a man caught in his own trap. In trying to unlock the mystery of Kit Randall, in attempting to teach her to want him, he'd come to want her.

Too much.

Now they were in a standoff. He had no doubt she'd leave as she'd threatened if he tried to make love to her again. Even though she wanted him, her Randall pride would force her to keep her word.

Alex muttered another curse, jerked his car keys from his pocket, and strode toward the Mercedes.

He'd take a long, fast ride and then he'd come back and work all day, maybe into the night if he had to. He'd work so hard he'd be too tired to think of making love to Kit. He'd let his work at the farm consume him, just as his work at Summit Enterprises had.

He was vaguely aware of the construction crew's startled faces turning towards him when he gunned the engine and roared away.

The pink-beige stucco and red-tile-roofed grandstand of Del Mar Race Track sparkled against its background of crystalline blue sky. The day was perfect, the track fast, and Copper King walked calmly into the saddling ring. He pricked his ears at the gaudily dressed, enthusiastic crowd that pressed against the low white fence surrounding the area. Many pointed and smiled at the colt. Others studied him carefully and marked their programs. Aware of their attention, Copper King arched his neck and lifted his forelegs into a paradelike prance.

Miguel gripped the colt's lead rope tighter and turned to wink at Kit. "Our boy's a real showoff."

"He sure is," she responded automatically. Everything was fine, she assured herself again, but she chewed her lower lip worriedly and her palms were slick with sweat. She dried them on the skirt of her blue sundress as unobtrusively as possible.

Hal Davis's rasping voice came from behind her. "You got some nerve entering a green colt in a race like this." He jerked Nightwatch's bridle, forcing the colt's delicate black head down. "But then you

Randalls always was crazy. Now you're workin' for that bastard Menendez.'' He took the stub of his cigar from his mouth and jabbed it at her, his lip curling in unconscious imitation of Blane. "We're goin' to show you today, lady. Nightwatch is the horse to beat in this race, but he ain't never been beat and no colt who likes to run into the rail is goin' to beat him. Not now and not ever.''

"I'm sure you believe that," Kit said evenly. "We'll just have to see, won't we?" She began to saddle Copper King, her back turned to Hal.

She'd just tightened the cinch when the jockeys strode into the ring. Tiny men, they were among the world's greatest athletes, and they walked with a confidence that conveyed their specialness, their brightly colored silks catching the sunlight. Some of them waved to the crowd. Others, like Copper King's jockey, Pat Knight, walked purposefully to their mounts.

His brow furrowed, Pat inspected the colt and nodded approvingly. "How do you want me to ride him, boss lady?''

"It's a short race. Get him to the front and keep him there.''

Pat's serious expression gave way to a slow smile that spread across his thin, weatherbeaten face. "I like that plan," he said, his blue eyes alight. "It's easy for an old country boy to understand.''

Shaking her head, Kit smiled back. Pat wasn't young and he didn't require simple instructions. He was one of the smartest and most talented jockeys in American racing, and she'd been flattered when he'd agreed to ride Copper King. Because they had not been run at a racetrack, the colt's blazing workouts were unofficial, but Pat had believed her when she'd told him Copper King's times. "A Randall's word is good as money in the bank," he'd said, and Kit had known he meant it. Then he'd told her a long story about how her father had helped him when he was a young jockey hustling for mounts. Oliver Randall had touched many lives, and if Copper King was half the horse she thought he was, her father would touch many more.

When the microphone blared "Riders up!" she stroked the colt's neck one last time for luck and helped Pat vault into the saddle. Pat waved his crop. "I'll try to bring him home ahead."

Kit waved back with a hand that trembled. "You do that."

When she turned to leave the ring, she was caught in a fierce blue gaze. Blane's nose had healed, but it wasn't perfect anymore. A look of hate froze his handsome features into a hard, evil expression she hadn't seen before. "Hello, Blane," she said, keeping her tone light.

He nodded curtly, his gaze never leaving her face, and when she tried to move away, he grabbed her arm. "I'll get Menendez for what he did to me. Today Nightwatch will beat your colt, but that will be only the beginning. I'll—"

"Do nothing except let go of Kit's arm before I break yours." Alex's voice slid silkily over them and his smile was fixed firmly in place. Only Kit and Blane had heard Alex's words. For all the people near them knew, they might have been three old friends chatting about the weather.

Blane released her, a look of fear shadowing his eyes. "You haven't heard the last of this," he said, and disappeared a moment later into the ivy-covered barn where Nightwatch was stabled.

Kit and Alex joined Jake and Consuelo Menendez at the edge of the crowd. "We saw it all," Jake said gleefully. "Maybe Blane'll watch the race on closed circuit TV from the barn. The Wentworth box is close to ours and that fella's awful scared of your nephew. Did you know that, Consuelo?"

Consuelo's silver-looped earrings glinted in the sunlight with the side-to-side movement of her head. "Alejandro knows that I do not approve of violence." She pointed to her coarse black hair threaded with white and drawn into a tight knot at the base of her neck. "More then one of these white hairs have come from Alejandro's fighting. I thought he left behind such foolishness when he was a boy."

Alex laughed, dropped an arm across Consuelo's plump, black-clad shoulders, and leaned far down to kiss the top of the tiny woman's head. "When I get conceited, my aunt feeds me a slice of humble pie."

"If it's as good as the rest of her cooking, I'd eat it and be happy." Jake winked at Consuelo and she beamed at him.

They were flirting! Kit knew she looked surprised, and she composed her expression. She'd been so busy getting the colt ready for the race she hadn't noticed the attraction between Jake and Consuelo or the new sparkle in Jake's eyes. His color was better, too, and he hadn't used his cane in days. In love again at seventy, was he? Kit liked the idea, but she felt a pang of regret, too. Jake didn't need her anymore. She had become the outsider.

Consuelo placed her hands on Kit's arm, and her liquid brown eyes were soft when she asked, "You are nervous about the race, no?"

"Nervous? I'm terrified!"

"Let's get up to the box where you can see the colt," Alex said.

Kit led the way to the Randall box, and by the time she was seated with Alex and Consuelo on either side of her, the horses were well into their warmup. Kit trained her binoculars on Copper King. He moved smoothly toward the starting gate, unperturbed by the crowd's noise and the presence of the other horses. "He looks fine," she said, and offered the binoculars to Consuelo.

She waved them away. "Keep them. I am too scared to look. Perhaps I will not watch the race at all."

"Just watch us and the Wentworth crowd," Jake said, indicating Marcella, Blane, and Hal Davis in the Wentworth box slightly below them and to their left. "We'll tell you all you need to know." He pointed at Nightwatch. "That black colt with the jockey in the red silks is their horse."

"*Sí*, the favorite of the crowd."

"He should be," Alex said. "He's a good colt—a proven performer."

Kit said nothing. She and Alex had argued long and hard about entering Copper King in this race, with Alex pointing out the colt's lack of experience as a reason for starting him at a lower level. In the end she'd won. She prayed she wouldn't regret winning the argument any more than she already did. Since then, Alex had avoided her, and in the rare moments when they'd accidentally met, he'd barely spoken. True, he'd been working like ten men, but he could at least be civil.

What was wrong with her? She'd threatened to run away if he didn't leave her alone. He'd done only what she'd demanded. Still, it hurt. Almost too much.

She raised the binoculars again and her forearm brushed Alex's shoulder. Tightness unrelated to her nervousness about the race gripped her chest like a vise and a shudder rippled through her, a helpless reaction she was powerless to contain.

The race. Concentrate on the race.

The horses had finished their warmup canter. "We'll know soon," she said, realizing she'd spoken only when Alex looked down at her.

"You've done all you can," he said. "I know that and I appreciate it."

"Maybe I *am* asking too much of him."

"As you said, we'll know soon." Alex smiled grimly when he tossed her words back at her.

Consuelo wrung her hands. "Not soon enough for me. No one told me that owning a race horse would be so hard."

Jake patted her hand. "It's harder for Kit. She and her daddy delivered the colt. Scarlet Princess had a bad time foaling him. Oliver and Kit thought they were going to lose her and the colt, too. Even the vet gave up on them, but Kit pulled them through.''

Alex stared at her. ''You did?''

Jake nodded emphatically. ''Darned right she did. Kit is the best horsewoman I've ever known, and believe me, I've known a lot of them. Why, I remember once—''

Kit shot him a desperate, quelling glance. ''Jake, please—''

He ignored her. ''When she was just a little girl, she started to spend all of her time in the barns, and—''

Kit tried again. ''Jake—''

''Let him talk, Kit,'' Alex commanded. ''I find his stories fascinating, particularly this one. We can listen and watch the horses.''

When Jake was nervous, he talked more than usual, and he told an interminable story with the young Kit Randall as its heroine. His words tumbled over each other faster and faster as Copper King approached the starting gate.

She dared to look at Alex again, cutting her eyes around and giving him a nervous, sidelong look. He was watching the horses as they were loaded into the gate, but it was clear that he was carefully listening to every word of Jake's story, too.

She heaved a resigned sigh and followed Alex's gaze. Nightwatch went into the gate first. He was followed by two colts and a filly—all long shots— then by Copper King and four other horses. The field of nine stood poised for a moment and an anticipatory hush fell over the crowd. Kit's stomach turned over.

The crowd roared as the horses bolted from the gate. Kit jumped up, screaming like the rest. Then her mind froze, her breath caught in her throat. Copper King was falling!

"No!" Consuelo screamed.

Pat Knight fell forward, his body angled over the colt's head. Reflexively, Pat grabbed Copper King's mane and threw himself backward, using all his weight and strength and skill to keep the colt upright. For a sickening instant, they were stopped, frozen in space and time, then the colt righted himself.

"Pat's done it!" Jake yelled. "They're in the race now!"

But the field was drawing away with each stride. Pat steadied the colt and urged him on.

"Our colt's not quitting!" Jake shouted.

"He won't quit!" Kit yelled above the crowd's roar. "He'll be beaten, but he won't quit!"

Copper King lengthened his stride, passing one horse, then two more. Four horses, nearly shoulder to shoulder, loomed in front of him, stretched across the inside of the track.

"He's blocked!" Jake's voice cracked. "Pat's going to have to take him the long way!"

Calmly, Pat checked the colt and moved him to the outside. For what seemed an eternity, Copper King and the others matched each other stride for stride, great muscles smoothing and bunching, slim legs blurring with vivid, stirring speed. Then Pat brought down his whip and Copper King zoomed away from the rest straight down the middle of the track, each long, fluid stride carrying him closer to the leader.

Nightwatch ran five lengths ahead of the field.

Marcella screamed her horse's name.

"Hang on, Nightwatch!" Blane pleaded.

Pat's crop arced down and somewhere deep inside him the big red colt found more speed.

Kit pounded Alex's arm. "Look at him go!"

"But he's too late!" Alex shouted.

"No! He's not too late!"

Great muscles straining, Copper King bore down on Nightwatch and together the two tearing, thundering colts and their frenzied, screaming jockeys pounded toward the wire. Twenty yards from the finish, Pat's whip flashed once, twice, and Copper King drew away.

There was a roar—a great, pulsating wave of sound. "He's won!" Kit screamed. "He's—"

Alex's kiss stopped her words.

EIGHT

Kit poured her second cup of coffee of the morning, nearly spilling it in her excitement. "Don't you see, Consuelo? It's not just that Copper King won the race. It's *how* he won it."

Holding the silver loving cup Copper King had been awarded, Jake performed a little two-step around the kitchen table. "And who he beat. Nightwatch was supposed to be the best two-year-old in the country." Jake set the cup down on the sideboard and caressed it with his gnarled hand. "Did you see the looks on Marci and Blane's faces? And that dadblamed Hal Davis could have killed us all."

Alex pulled out a chair for Jake and gestured him into it, then sat down himself, "It's nice to beat the Wentworths, but I want to know what we're going to do next." For the first time since he'd kissed her,

Alex looked directly at Kit. "What are your plans for the colt?"

She wet her lips, suddenly nervous. "Everybody with a good three-year-old entertains fantasies about the first Saturday in May."

Consuelo looked bewildered. "What happens at that time?"

"The Kentucky Derby," Jake said, chuckling while Kit cringed. He knew that she didn't like those words said aloud when they had a colt they might enter in the race. He said them again more emphatically to tease her. "*The Kentucky Derby*. Kit's awful superstitious about that race. She figures if we say its name, it'll jinx the horse we enter."

Consuelo's generous lips thinned. "Copper King is good enough to overcome any jinx. But he is only two, is he not?"

Alex watched Kit narrowly. "Like all thoroughbreds he'll have an official birthday on January first. At least Kit will be around for that." His voice was harsh and low.

Consuelo's mouth formed into a small O of surprise. "You are still planning to leave even now that Copper King has done so well?"

Kit nodded. "The last day in January," she said, avoiding Alex's gaze. She knew if she looked at him he'd read the sadness in her eyes. "By then, Copper King will have had the best start I know how to give him and Jake will be strong enough to take over the colt's training."

Abruptly Alex pushed his chair back from the table, the wood shrieking a protest against the tile floor. "If you three will excuse me, I have a lot of work to do."

Jake slanted him a surprised look. "But we haven't firmed up the plans for the colt."

"Later." Alex tossed the word over his shoulder as he strode toward the door.

Consuelo waited until she could no longer hear Alex's thudding footsteps on the porch before she expelled her breath. "He did not even have breakfast," she said, shaking her head so that her silver earrings bounced against her jawline. "Alejandro works too hard and he does not care for himself." She dropped her hands on her ample hips. "I had hoped that his life would be different now that he has his first real home."

"Didn't he have a home in San Francisco?" Jake asked.

"A penthouse with one of those million-dollar views. The decorator made the place look like an art gallery instead of a home—all marble and black leather with paintings and statues that looked like the work of *niños*—children." Consuelo waved a small hand in a gesture that took in the house. "But this—this is a home—a place for wife and children. This is what Alejandro has needed ever since I found him."

Kit's lips opened, but it was Jake who broke the sudden silence. "He told me you'd found him, but he didn't say how or where."

Consuelo smiled, her brown eyes soft with memories. "Thirty-four years ago, when Alejandro was three or four, I found him outside my house in my small village in Mexico. He looked like one of those dolls you put in the fields.''

Jake eyes Consuelo intently. "A scarecrow."

"*Sí*, a scarecrow. He was hungry and cold and he had bruises all over him, as if someone had beaten him. I was young and my husband was dead and my two *niños* were hungry"—Consuelo spread her hands, palms up—"but what could I do? I could not let him starve, so I took him into my own home, poor as it was."

"You never found his parents?" Jake asked.

"My village was poor. Many children roamed the streets, I have seen them day after day growing dirtier and thinner, their hands always outstretched. No one claims them. Almost no one notices them." Consuelo's dark eyes warmed. "But something about Alejandro made him different from the rest. Maybe it was those gray eyes too big for his face, or maybe it was because he stood apart from the rest and refused to beg. Whatever it was, when my sister brought my family and me to the United States, Alejandro came with us to the home of his father.''

Kit made no attempt to hide her interest. She leaned against the counter, her arms folded across her chest, her gaze intent. "How do you know his father was an American?"

"Alejandro is bigger than my people. His skin is fairer." Consuelo's earrings danced again. "And no one in my part of Mexico has eyes like his."

Jake stirred his coffee even though Kit knew it must be cold. "It must be tough not to know your daddy," he said finally.

Consuelo took an immaculate white apron from a drawer and put it on over her brightly flowered dress. "I think Alejandro's father was a college student who came to Mexico in the spring for a week of drinking and partying. Like so many others he left something behind that he didn't know about—that he was never to know about. Maybe that is why Alejandro's mother did not want him. His presence made her feel shame."

Consuelo lifted her chin and a patch of white skin under it quivered. "For a while, when he was older, Alejandro shamed me, too. He fought and got into trouble at school. Then he left school to work and after a time he came here." She smiled at Kit. "This is where his fortune changed. Here was beauty and peace and order. Here he met your father."

Not trusting her voice, Kit simply nodded.

Consuelo looked at her for a long moment. "For a while after he bought this place, Alejandro was happy, but now he is"—she lifted her shoulders, seeking a word—"troubled, and he will not tell me why. That is not like him." She stared straight at Kit.

"I . . . I have no idea of what could be wrong with Alex."

"I did not say that you did," Consuelo replied gently. She prepared cereal, toast, and fruit juice for Jake, who accepted them without complaint, and prepared a breakfast of sausage and scrambled eggs for herself and Kit.

Kit wasn't hungry, but she ate everything on her plate to appease Consuelo. "Thank you, Consuelo," she said, rising from the table. "That was wonderful, but I have to get down to the barn."

Jake stood. "I'll go with you. The boys will want to hear about the race."

"You go ahead, Jake," Consuelo said. "I would like to talk with Kit for a little while." Seeing his curious expression, she added, "Woman talk."

Seemingly satisfied with her explanation, Jake left, whistling an off-key version of "Camptown Races."

Consuelo's charming smile wrapped Kit close. "You are so proud of that beautiful horse. You worked hard to bring him this far."

She nodded. Consuelo was leading up to something, and Kit wasn't sure she wanted to hear it. She began to carry her dishes to the sink.

"You and Alejandro were excited when Copper King won the race—so excited that you kissed."

"Alex kissed *me*," Kit responded defensively.

"But you liked it." Kit's cheeks flamed and Consuelo said more mildly, "Just for a minute. Then you and Alejandro jumped apart as if you had been burned. For the rest of the afternoon, you were not near each other again. You made sure to keep people between you, and yet"—Consuelo's voice grew very soft—"your eyes found each other, just as they always do."

Kit's embarrassment was complete. It flamed down her neck and shoulders. She could even feel the heat of it in her stomach. "I . . . like Alex," she said in a low, stupid, little girl's voice that came from high in her throat.

Consuelo was silent so long that Kit began to wonder if she'd heard. Then the older woman said, "I think it is more than that—for both of you. I have seen Alejandro with other women. He smiled, he teased them, he was fond of them, but they could not hurt him by telling him they would leave. They could not drive him from the room. Only you can do that." The smallest hint of a smile warmed her eyes, but it did not touch her lips. "I never thought that I would see my nephew in—what do the soldiers say?—full retreat? And from a woman."

The adrenaline that had flowed through Kit since Copper King won the race dissipated in an instant, leaving her exhausted and weak. "Alex is used to getting his own way. He wants me here until he . . . tires of me."

"He would not have said that."

"*I* said that. Alex denies it, of course."

"Why can you not take him at his word?" Consuelo cocked her head to one side and eyed Kit shrewdly. "And why is it so hard for you to share whatever burden it is that you carry?"

Kit felt a nervous laugh gather in her throat and she swallowed it. "You sound just like Jake," she said in as steady a voice as she could manage.

"Jake is a wise man."

Kit tried to shrug carelessly, to throw out a hand in a studiedly casual gesture. "Sometimes he's wrong."

"This time he is not wrong, and I am not wrong. All my life I have studied people. I know when they have trouble even when they are proud and brave like you and try to pretend that they are happy. I would help you, Kit. Alejandro would help you.''

Kit was so tired she ached with fatigue. It seemed to push itself into every crevice of her body and her skin seemed to swell with it. "How could he help me even if he wanted to? By writing a check? It's too late for that. Besides, there are things more important than money—things like my father's reputation, like—'' She gave a small gasp of horror and, too late, placed her hand in front of her mouth to stop her words.

Slow comprehension bloomed in Consuelo's eyes. Outside, Alex shouted to one of the workmen and the woman's gaze moved in the direction of the sound. The silence stretched between them for a moment, then Consuelo said, "I will say nothing of this. Nothing at all.''

The next morning Matilda nuzzled Kit's cheek and she emerged slowly and reluctantly from sleep. "Just a few minutes more, Kitty," she murmured, her speech slurring, her eyes drifting shut again. She let the warm heavy tide draw her back under.

Matilda nudged Kit again and meowed close to her ear. "Oh, all right," she sighed, "I'll let you out, but it's awfully early. What's wrong with you, anyway?" She threw her legs over the side of the bed and stumbled to the door with Matilda preceding her. The instant she opened the door the cat raced through it and rushed down the dark stairs.

Kit returned to bed, but she couldn't fall asleep again. Mentally she reviewed every move she'd make in training Copper King. For almost an hour, she managed to hold her other thoughts at bay and then, exhausted, she let them plummet to the center of her mind. An awful guilt flooded her. True, she'd been exhausted when she'd talked with Consuelo, her mind slow-moving with fatigue, but her betrayal of her father was inexcusable.

Kit got out of bed and began to pace the tiny, hot room, her arms crossed in front of her. "Luckily for you, Consuelo will keep your secret," she muttered into the first gray light of dawn. "She's not going to let anything hurt Alex."

Kit felt a headache begin to bear down on her with steel jaws. *Not again*, she thought. *Not today*. She'd promised Alex that they'd meet to discuss the colt. As always when she dealt with him, she needed her wits about her. She laughed mirthlessly at the thought. If she'd had her wits about her, she'd never have let him kiss her . . . make love to her . . .

In an instant every detail of their lovemaking sprang vividly to her mind and a spiraling sensation began low in her stomach. She felt dizzy and disoriented, drunk on and excited by the memory. She put her hand on the window sill to steady herself and rested her forehead against the glass. Her anger had masked her shyness and Alex's throaty, urgent sounds had muffled her tiny cry of pain. He thought she was a sophisticated woman of the world. What would he think if he learned she'd been a virgin?

Her headache increased and the all-too familiar pounding blurred her vision. Looking out the window toward the barns, she blinked her eyes to clear them.

Above the barn where the horses were stabled, she saw an orange glow in the sky.

Halfway down the path, Kit heard the horses screaming. She stumbled and threw out her hands to break her fall. Her palms skidded painfully on the dirt and her knee slammed down hard on a rock. Ignoring the pain, she thrust herself upright and ran toward the open barn doors.

Black smoke billowed around Miguel as he emerged from the barn leading Moonscape. Straining against the lead rope, the fear-crazed mare tried to run back toward the flames. Miguel ran a short distance, dragging her behind him. Screaming, urging her away from the fire, he slashed a rope across her side. The mare reared, hesitated, then wheeled and ran toward the safety of the paddocks.

More mares appeared through the smoke, driven by shouting, cursing grooms who lashed at them with bridles and ropes and boards—with anything that would make them more afraid of the men than of the flames. Ears pinned, eyes rolling, Scarlet Princess, the dominant mare, turned back toward the barn. Shouting and waving his arms, the smallest groom jumped into her path. An instant before she reached him, Scarlet Princess wheeled and ran toward the paddocks. The other mares circled blindly, then, obeying an instinct as old as time, galloped after their leader.

Kit raced forward. "Where's Copper King?" she yelled above the roar of the flames.

"Still in there!" Miguel's eyes were red in his

soot-blackened face. "The others are out, but we couldn't get to him!"

"I'll get him!"

"He's too close to the fire!" Miguel grabbed her arm and managed to hold her for an instant before she twisted away and dashed toward the barn. "Don't, Miss Kit!"

She plunged inside and instantly her lungs felt seared, hers eyes smarted, and tears rolled down her face. She grabbed a towel from a rack beside the door, thrust it into a water trough, and draped the dripping towel around her head and shoulders.

Flames ate along the side of the barn. Above her head beams burned and fire spread along the roof, sending great tentacles toward its peak. Fear gripped her throat. *Soon.* The word pounded in her ears. *She'd have to get to him soon.*

Coughing, nauseated, she stumbled forward, squinting through billowing smoke dyed by the flames like fog tinted by headlights. The skin of her hands was so hot she slapped first at one, then at the other, thinking for a panicky instant that her skin had caught fire. She listened for the colt's terrified whinnies and the thudding of his hooves, but she heard nothing over the roar of the flames and the pounding of blood in her ears.

A chunk of flaming debris fell and she jumped away from it, taking a deep breath, inhaling more smoke and with it the stench of burning leather and wood. She bent low and struggled on. Behind her, a rafter fell in a roaring golden explosion of sparks. The middle section of the bank of stalls to her left burst into flames. She lurched on and at last heard Copper King's anguished shrieks and thudding hooves.

She fell, crawled forward, and tried not to think about dying. She reached Copper King's stall, pulled herself upright, and yanked the door open. Eyes rolling, Copper King reared, his hoofs slashing near her face. She threw up her hands, made a frantic leap for his halter and hung on, her feet dangling. She freed a hand, threw the towel over his eyes, and clutched it in a clump beneath his jaw. Unable to see the flames, the colt calmed a little and, still clutching the towel, Kit dragged him from the stall.

Kit's eyes stung. She couldn't see. Trying not to breathe, she lurched on, the colt following at a manic trot. Her mind floated and the world began to ooze away from her.

A rafter above her head crackled and roared and a red-orange shower of sparks fell on her and Copper King. The colt skittered to the side, twisting her arm and shoulder. She stiffened as if shot through with electricity, and for a moment her mind focused. She had to get under the rafter that had fallen across the center aisle of the barn. And to hurry. She had to hurry . . .

She fought for air and inhaled smoke. She tripped and fell to her knees. She struggled to her feet and fell down again. Twisting her hand in the colt's mane, she forced his head down near the floor where the air was clearer. Copper King was suddenly, ominously, passive. Soon he'd be overcome by smoke, as she would. *Faster*. Her lips formed the word, but she heard no sound above the crackle and roar of the flames.

Limply, with no more than the shadow of an instinct, she crawled forward.

Alex grabbed the front of Miguel's shirt and lifted the groom off his feet. "She's *where*?"

"In the barn! She went after Copper King!"

Cursing wildly, Alex thrust Miguel aside and sprinted toward the barn. Damn the woman! As beautiful and talented as the colt was, he wasn't worth her life. Alex jerked a wet towel from one of the men and wrapped it around his head as he ran.

He took a deep breath and plunged inside only to have the heat send him reeling back. He caught himself, lowered his head, and willed himself to move forward. The ceiling and one wall of the barn were on fire. A few feet ahead of him, a flaming twenty-foot beam had fallen across the barn's center aisle, one end still attached to the roof support, the other resting on the floor. He'd have to duck under the high end and hope the damn thing didn't give way before he got Kit out.

He lurched ahead. The heat intensified and the smoke thickened. *If* he got Kit out. He gritted his teeth and willed away the thought. He *had* to save her.

He ducked under the beam and a shower of sparks landed on him. Yanking the towel from his head, he managed to smother them, but he inhaled a lungful of smoke. Instantly he felt lightheaded. *Soon, my darling. I've got to find you soon.*

He squinted through the smoke and flames and saw a black shape looming ahead. Copper King, his head down, a white towel shielding his eyes and trailing down one side of his neck, wobbled on unsteady legs.

Kit's voice came from near the floor. "Alex, help me."

He blinked his stinging eyes to bring her into focus, but she remained a dark shape obscured by his blurred vision and the thick black layers of smoke. Alex tried to say her name, but managed only a croak. He swallowed hard and forced out, "I'm here. I'll help." He wasn't sure she heard him. He dropped to his knees to lift her. "Let go of the colt."

"No."

"We'll all die, Kit. Let him go."

"Then . . . save yourself." She inched forward, her grip tight as death on Copper King's mane.

Alex yanked the towel from her face and wrapped it around her head. "I'm not leaving without you."

"Both . . . of us."

Alex's legs and arms felt like lead. "Both of you then."

Her lips formed words, but Alex couldn't hear them. He stumbled under her weight. He'd always thought of her as tiny, light, almost fragile, but now she was heavy . . . so heavy.

He had to get out.

He could think of nothing else.

Lightheaded.

The firey rafter was in front of him again, the wall

to his right enveloped in flames. He shook his head to clear it. The opening between the burning wall and the rafter was too narrow for the three of them. He stopped, trying to puzzle out the problem with a brain that moved too slowly. Kit lay against his chest, close to his heart.

A firefighter wouldn't carry her this way.

Think.

Our lives depend on it.

She gave a small grunt of surprise when he swung her over his shoulder. He placed his right arm over the back of her knees. Pull the horse along . . . behind . . . us. We'll go through single . . . file.

Alex reached behind him, grabbed one of Copper King's cheek straps, and lurched forward on rubbery legs. Just in front of the rafter, he hunched over, pulled Kit closer, and launched himself through the narrow, fiery opening, dragging the colt behind him.

His momentum carried them several feet on the other side. He sprawled on the floor, Kit atop him. Her head slammed into his and she gave a small groan of pain. Alex released the colt and struggled to his feet, swaying under Kit's weight.

His heart beat at an incredible rate and his lungs burned. He could barely see anymore, could hear nothing but the fire's roar. He was going to die. The last bit of his strength was flowing away, unstoppable.

Kit moved in his arms and his mind focused again. If he died, she would, too.

She couldn't die. He wouldn't *let* her die. He took a slow, agonizing step, then another.

Sunlight.

A wisp of cooler air.

He staggered out of the barn and fell to his knees, holding on to Kit with the last bit of his ebbing strength.

Kit breathed greedily, filling her lungs, letting her brain clear, opening her eyes to the light of a crystalline morning. She was alive! She experienced a quick rush of joy, then a stab of fear. Jake, frowning, bent over her . . . Consuelo, her face serious . . . a sooty-faced fireman . . . "Alex?" Kit asked in a raw, rasping voice..

"He's fine." Jake's frown gave way to a bright smile. "And the colt's OK, too. He's just singed in spots and a little woozy."

The fireman nodded in the direction of the still-smoking barn. "As soon as Mr. Menendez found out you'd be all right, he organized your employees and neighbors into a fire-fighting brigade. The fire was almost under control when we got here."

Jake's grin widened. "That Alex . . ."

Consuelo's dark-brown eyes gleamed with pride. "He is some man, my nephew."

Silently Kit agreed. Through half-closed eyes, she saw Alex appear around the corner of the barn with three of their neighbors. They were all wealthy and powerful men, but their posture conveyed their deference to Alex as clearly as words.

She sat up, knuckling her eyes. "I can help now . . . do *something*."

"You've already done something. You saved that beautiful horse." The fireman placed a hand on her shoulder to hold her in place. "Now you can relax. Everything's under control."

"I didn't save Copper King. Alex did. He saved me, too," she announced, looking at the three of them defiantly, even though she knew they wouldn't argue the point.

"Let us go home, Kit," Consuelo said. "You can bathe and rest."

She *was* bone-tired, her throat raw as an open wound, her body filthy and sore and reeking of smoke, her hair thick with ashes and soot. Her gaze sought Alex again, but he'd disappeared into a group of men crowded around one of the fire trucks pouring water on the barn. The fire was under control, and only a few pennants of smoke still curled skyward. She nodded to Consuelo. "It's over anyway."

Jake ensconced himself on a shaded bench to watch the mopping-up operation and Consuelo accompanied Kit back to the house. She sat on the bed and took shallow, painful breaths while the older woman drew water in the old-fashioned claw-footed tub that took up most of the bathroom. When Consuelo turned off the tap, Kit moved painfully to the bathroom door.

"Shall I stay with you?" Consuelo asked.

"I can manage alone."

"I will go then. Jake and Alejandro have not yet had breakfast. I will fix yours later."

"I won't have time to eat. After I bathe I have to make arrangements for the horses."

"Alejandro will take care of everything."

"But I'm responsible for the horses, not Alex."

For a moment Consuelo looked as if she'd like to argue, but she shrugged and said, "I will be back to check on you in a little while."

Consuelo had filled the hot, steaming bath with bubbles, and as soon as she left, Kit began to work her way out of her filthy clothes, every muscle moaning a protest. She lowered herself gingerly into the fragrant water and gave a little sigh of contentment. She closed her eyes and let the water unclench her muscles. Her mind went blank, floating between sleep and wakefulness.

When the water cooled, she roused herself and used her toes to turn on the tap and warm the water again, her movements languid. The room swam back into focus.

Alex had risked his life to save her.

She was used to seeing people do almost impossibly brave things—thoroughbred racing carried with it the constant risk of death or injury—but Alex's courage staggered her. His bravery was all the more impressive because it was impersonal. He'd have risked his life for anybody.

"Jake and Consuelo are right. You're quite a man, Alex Menendez," she whispered. "Quite a man."

"I'm glad you think so."

Startled, she sat up abruptly, then just as quickly slid under the water. The thick bubbles were now only tiny islands of foam clinging to the edges of the tub, and if Alex came closer and looked down at her, her naked body would be clearly visible under the water.

He came closer.

In fact, he sat down on the edge of the tub. He loomed above her, seeming even larger than she remembered. His eyes were red-rimmed, his face soot-blackened. He smelled of ashes and smoke and his hair was dull with them.

He was gorgeous.

Kit's body and face flamed with embarrassment and she sank lower in the water. "I—I didn't hear you come in."

"Evidently." His smile was even whiter in his darkened face. His gaze raked her. "How are you feeling?"

She told herself she wouldn't try to hide her nakedness with her hands, no matter how much she was tempted, but she had to shift positions. His scrutiny was embarrassing her, making her restless. She grabbed the bottle of shampoo Consuelo had placed beside the tub and began to lather her hair, arching her body so that her face turned down, toward the water. "I'm fine," she said, her voice muffled. "Just fine."

"There's that Randall pride again. God forbid you should admit you hurt like other people."

"I don't suppose *you* hurt," she said, glancing combatively at him through the thick screen of her soapy hair.

"On the contrary. I hurt like hell—in places I didn't know I had." He hesitated a moment, then began to roll back his sleeves. "Let me help with that." He pushed away her hands and began to rub her scalp.

"I'm perfectly capable of washing my own hair."

"But think of how much more fun it is to have me do it." His voice was slow and soft.

He kneaded her scalp and she felt a smile of involuntary pleasure curve her mouth. He was right, she thought, nearly purring. It *was* more fun to have him wash her hair. She closed her eyes again, feeling her muscles loosen, her body grow slack and warm. "Mmmmm," she said, in spite of herself.

Alex turned on the tap. "Dip your head."

She inclined her head beneath the stream of water and he rinsed the soapsuds from it. "I can wash your body, too, if you like." There was a teasingly hopeful note in his voice and he raised his eyebrows quizzically. For an instant Kit had a clear mental picture of his large, beautiful hands, slick with soap, sliding over her body. She felt a powerful jolt somewhere in the core of her. "That . . . won't be necessary." She looked at him for a long, quiet moment. Then she heard the sound of her own voice. "I can bathe—"

"Yourself. Of course you can. I just thought it might be more . . . interesting if I did it for you." He grinned lecherously. "Or we could bathe together."

The mental picture his statement evoked made her breathing grow labored and shallow. She tried to smile, to force a light, teasing note into her voice. "Your aunt said she'd be back to check on me. What would she think if she found us in the tub together?"

"That I'm a lucky man. She likes you, Kit. More than that, she respects and admires you."

"She actually *respects* a lazy rich girl who sold her birthright?"

"She sees more than that in you, and so do I—now." She shivered—whether from nervousness or the coolness of the water, she couldn't be sure, but Alex noticed it and said, "You need to get out of there." He paused for a heartbeat. "Shall I help you?"

She looked down at the edge of the tub, where his filthy jeans had left a faint rim of soot. "I . . . can manage."

"I'll wait in your room, then."

She ducked her head in acknowledgment and waited until the door closed behind him before she rose from the water and drew on the white terry-cloth robe that always hung behind the bathroom door. She belted it tightly around her and stepped hesitantly into the bedroom.

Hipshot, arms folded across his broad chest, Alex stood by the window. "I want you to take the day off. You look like you could use some sleep."

"The horses—"

"The neighbors have volunteered to care for them until the new barn is ready. The Lansings have already taken Copper King. I've sent Miguel with him." Alex dropped his large hands to his side and they tightened there. "You were right about my needing the neighbors. They got here faster than the fire department did, and some of them did impossibly brave things."

"You were the bravest of all." Kit's voice was husky and scratched in her swollen throat. "You saved my life . . . Copper King's life. Thank you, Alex."

"If you hadn't brought the colt halfway out, we wouldn't have made it." Alex shook his head in wonder. "Your courage and your love for that colt takes my breath away."

Not trusting her voice, she said nothing.

"Why did you sell him, Kit?" Alex moved close and looked down at her until she lifted her gaze to his. "*Why?*"

"I—"

The front door slammed.

"Consuelo's here," Kit said, relief washing through her.

"I'll have to speak to my aunt about her timing." His narrowed gaze made Kit's heart pound harder. "But we're not finished with this conversation, Kit. Not until I know everything."

"I've told you everything!" she protested.

"I don't think you have. I think I've stripped away another layer of Kit Randall, but I haven't gotten to the core of her yet." He brushed her mouth with a kiss. "And I won't quit until I know everything. You can bet on that."

NINE

Two days later, almost everyone who'd helped fight the fire in the old barn was gathered at a party in the still-unfinished new one. Alex stood by the door, smiling and shaking hands with his guests. The mariachi band on the stage at the far end of the cavernous space struck a crashing, discordant note and he winced, arching his eyebrows at Charles and Caroline Lansing, who'd just arrived.

Caroline stuck out a slim hand, then stood on tiptoe to kiss his cheek. "Sometimes bein' tone deaf like Charles is an advantage," she said in her soft Virginia drawl. "But don't you worry. This is goin' to be a wonderful party. And it was so sweet of you to give it for all the people who helped you fight the fire."

"It was Kit's idea." Kit was standing near one of the four heavily laden buffet tables bisecting the enormous space. She was in animated conversation with an interesting cross-section of guests—a fireman, two construction workers, the fabulously wealthy owner of one of Solway's finest farms and his wife, a former Las Vegas showgirl. From time to time, Kit looked in Alex's direction, but he knew better than to expect she'd come to him. He'd have to wait for a chance to get away from the people who'd crowded around him all evening before he could go to her. He smiled down at Caroline. "Kit planned the party, too. She and my Aunt Consuelo prepared all the food."

"Kit gives such good parties," Caroline said. "I remember one she gave when she was working at Sheik Muhammed's stud farm in the south of France that was the hit of the social season."

"When was that?" Alex asked sharply.

Caroline pursed her lips and frowned. "I don't remember exactly. I think it was the year after she graduated from the Sorbonne. She spent the followin' year at that big farm in England, and worked at Count Andoral's farm in Spain after that. I'd have thought she'd have told you."

So that was how she'd spent her years in Europe! "Kit says almost nothing about herself," he said, hiding his surprise. "I've pried some of the facts of her life out of her, but it's like pulling teeth. She's mysterious."

"That's one way of puttin' it. *I've* always thought of the Randalls as possessin' great dignity, and dignified people don't make their affairs public. We southerners admire that quality," Caroline said, drawing herself up a little.

Charles smiled fondly at his wife. "They admire the quality, but like the rest of us they don't hesitate for a moment to try to find out everyone's business."

While Alex and Charles laughed, Caroline playfully slapped her husband's arm. "That's part of the sport, darlin'."

"And my wife plays it well. Over the years, she's managed to accumulate information about everyone. The FBI could learn a lot from her." Charles's blue eyes narrowed in mock-serious threat. "So beware of her."

"Why was Kit working at those farms?" Alex asked as casually as he could manage. "Was she just sticking with something familiar until she could decide what she wanted to do with her life?"

"Good heavens, no!" Caroline said. "Kit has never wanted to do anything but raise horses." Caroline seemed horrified that he would even suggest such a thing and looked at Charles for confirmation. "She stayed in Europe to study at some of the best farms in the world. She and Oliver were going to—"

Charles took her arm. "Darling, I think the van Hazeltines would like to speak with us."

Caroline stared at Charles for a moment, then said, "Of . . . course. If you'll just excuse us, Alex. We haven't talked to Lauren and Barbara in ages."

Alex watched them go. Unless he missed his guess, he'd learn nothing more about Kit from either of them. Clearly, Charles hadn't wanted his wife to say as much as she had. Only his excellent manners had prevented him from hauling her away earlier.

A small smile played along Alex's lips. That Kit hadn't led the life of a jetsetter came as no real surprise. The more he'd learned about her, the more he'd realized how hard-working and conscientious she was. During those four years she'd been methodically preparing to go into partnership with Oliver at Randall Farm.

She'd never wanted to do anything else. Those words beat at him as he made his way across the crowded floor to the place where he'd last spotted Kit.

She wasn't there. She'd probably seen him coming and mingled with the crowd to avoid him, as she had since the day of the fire.

Now he knew why.

Sooner or later, if he'd kept pressing her, she'd have admitted why she sold the farm. Now she didn't have to. There was only one possible explanation. "You couldn't afford it anymore, could you, Kit?" he muttered as he threaded his way through the crowd.

"And your damned Randall pride kept you from telling me."

Three times in the next hour Alex spotted Kit and started toward her. Each time he was stopped by one of the guests and found himself playing the role of perfect host—laughing at jokes he'd already heard or that weren't funny or both, pretending interest in topics that didn't interest him, all the time seething with impatience to talk to Kit.

He was smiling down at a short, round woman and her almost equally short, plump husband when the band played a fanfare and the room quieted. Charles Lansing stepped to the microphone, his gaze finding Alex in the crowded room.

Charles held up a glass of champagne. "I'd like to propose a toast." As if by magic waiters appeared and passed among the guests, who took champagne-filled glasses from silver trays. "To our host, Alex Menendez, who is making Randall Farm beautiful again. His courage and leadership during the fire were an inspiration to us all." Charles smiled his enchanting smile. "Welcome to the neighborhood, Alex."

"Hear! Hear!" someone shouted, and they all turned to Alex, raising their glasses.

A lump tightened Alex's throat. For the first time in his restless, rootless life, he had a home.

He wished Kit had one, too.

Kit sat in the dappled moonlight under the ancient oak where she'd first seen Alex, the skirt of her white sundress spread around her. She smelled the lingering odor of smoke from the ruin of the barn rising like a giant black skeleton next to the stark white splendor of the new barn. She shivered a little, not from cold—the night was warm with only a faint breeze blowing from the east—but from the memory linked to that odor. She and Alex and Copper King had come so close to death!

That was why her senses were so sharp tonight. She brushed her fingers over the warm grass and it seemed that she touched every blade; she leaned against the trunk of the oak and felt it rough and solid against her back. Overhead an owl hooted and she cocked her head toward the sound.

A faint, sad smile curved her lips. She'd avoided Alex during the party. He was too good at battering her defenses, at stripping away the layers until he came frighteningly close to the truth. Someday, in a moment of weakness, she might blurt it out. "But I can't hurt you, my darling," she whispered. "I couldn't bear to hurt you."

She rested her head against the trunk and closed her eyes. She'd always loved the farm best at night, when all the others were sleeping. For a while she floated, almost asleep. Then her eyes jerked open. Alex was walking along the path toward the ruined barn. She sat very still and hoped he wouldn't notice her.

"Kit, is that you?"

"Y-yes."

He walked toward her. "You were going to let me walk by without saying a word. I might have, too, if I hadn't seen your white dress." He loomed over her, casting her in deep shadow. "Can't you sleep?"

"I haven't tried. I was enjoying the night. It's so beautiful and warm."

He sat beside her, leaning back, and rested his weight on his elbows, his long legs stretched out in front of him. "Yes," he said. "It is beautiful."

They were silent for a few moments, and then she said, "The party went well, I think."

"It was a wonderful party, except that you avoided me all evening."

She looked up the sloping lawn toward the house, its long, sweeping shape barely visible in the soft glow of moonlight. She couldn't deny what Alex said, so she didn't answer him.

"Caroline Lansing said something very interesting about you tonight."

"Oh?"

"She said that after college you worked on some of the best horse farms in Europe—that you never wanted to do anything but raise horses."

She tried to meet his eyes steadily, but her gaze dropped to her lap, where her hands fluttered nervously. "I—"

"There's only one reason why you'd have let the farm get into the condition it was in, and why you'd sell it and the horses." He reached out and lifted her chin, forcing her to raise her gaze to his. "You had money trouble. You were forced to sell out." When Kit didn't answer him, he said, "That's the reason, isn't it?"

Slowly she nodded.

"Why didn't you file chapter eleven? It would have given you time to reorganize . . . to get Copper King to the track."

"Randalls don't file for bankruptcy."

He sighed—a long, heartfelt sigh that slumped his broad shoulders. "I wonder how I knew you were going to say that?"

She just looked at him, her lips thinning.

He lay back full-length on the grass, folded his hands across his waist, and closed his eyes. Several minutes later, when she'd decided he was asleep and she was preparing to slip quietly away, he took her hand. "Stay with me a little longer, Kit."

And she did—almost relaxed at first, with the soft, warm breeze velvet against her skin, the perfume of sage and newly cut grass around her, then with increasing tension when Alex pulled her down against his chest and wrapped his arms around her.

He stroked her hair. "How proud you are . . . and how it must have hurt you to lose everything." She felt his lips against her cheek. "I want to take away the hurt, *querida*," he said against her ear.

Darling. Had he really called her *darling?* Desire crashed over her like a tidal wave and she pressed against him. He held her for a moment, held her hard, and then reversed their positions, his large body half on, half off hers as he gazed down at her face. "I've dreamed of holding you like this, of making love to you on the grass."

She wound her arms around his neck and brought his mouth down to meet hers. She shouldn't do this, she told herself.

She should not.

But she was caught in one of the most vivid, beautiful dreams of her life and she was powerless to resist it—to resist *him*. He ran a hand down her from her breast to the curve of her buttocks and back again to the strap of her sundress. He pushed it down, then its mate, reached slowly around her to find the zipper of her dress and slide it down.

Surely she would awaken from the dream soon.

But she didn't want to awaken.

Alex hooked a thumb over her bodice and slid her dress down until it pooled around her sandaled feet. She kicked it and her shoes aside, all the while encouraging him with lips and tongue and voice and caressing hands. He unhooked her strapless bra and tossed it away, stripped off her panties with a sweep of a large, warm hand.

She lay naked, lit by moonlight, under his passionate gaze. "You're so beautiful," Alex breathed, rising to strip away his clothes. From the comfort and security of her dream she watched him undress, his movements swift and frantic, his eyes glazed with desire.

He's like a nature god, she thought dimly. For an instant he stood above her, feet planted in the thick grass, legs corded like young trees, massive torso silvered in the moon's light. Then he lay beside her again, his throbbing arousal against her hip. He gathered her into his arms, murmuring "*Querida, querida*" as his breath fanned her ear and cheek. "I want to touch you all over, to explore every part of you, to make this a night we'll always remember."

Trembling began as he slid his hands down her cheeks and neck and shoulders, then to her arms and waist and hip and thighs. Her breath caught in her throat.

Her trembling intensified when his fingers moved around her nipples, his hands slid around her breasts, raised them to his lips. He took them one at a time into his mouth and flicked his tongue across them with mothlike lightness. She felt them harden.

She held his head between her hands, her thumbs against his cheeks, her fingers around the smooth curve of his neck and skull. She pressed him against her and murmured unintelligible words of encouragement and need, moving her head restlessly from side to side, her eyes closed, her lips parted, her breathing swift and shallow.

She felt him nudge her legs apart and kneel between them. Through the thick screen of her lashes she saw him arc above her, his hair tipped with silver, his strong face cast into shadow. His hands stroked her inner thighs, then went lightly, gently, between them, lingering there, seeking and finding the soft, warm core of her. Flame shot up her torso, down her legs. Her arms felt loose in their sockets, and a soft moan, light as a zephyr, escaped her open lips.

She reached down with tentative fingers to touch his maleness, heard his animal groan, and emboldened, began a slow, rhythmic stroking. He matched her rhythm until she thought she could stand no more.

But there *was* more.

She felt him draw away for an instant, then place his warm lips where his fingers had been, kissing, sucking, rolling her soft, moist flesh between lips and tongue. Fire ran through her, burned her with its heat. Her body tensed, convulsed, and she cried out her release.

"That," Alex whispered brokenly, "was for you, and this—*this* is for both of us."

He took her hands and guided them back to the smooth, warm hardness of him. She felt her frantic hands pulling him . . . pulling his hardness into the slick, hot emptiness of her. She raised her arms to drag him down to her, to feel some of his great weight pressed on her. "You're so little," he said. "I'm afraid I'll crush you."

"No . .. " The word ended in a little squeak of desire and momentary frustration.

Then he was against her, his chest hairs brushing her breasts, his massive body warming her. She felt the soft, sweet exploration of his hands on her stomach and breasts and thighs, thrilled to his tongue probing her mouth, the soft words he whispered in her ear.

The sweet slow rhythm began and built. He lifted himself on stiffened arms and rocked, and rocked. She dug her fingers into the hard flesh of his back, encouraging him with touch and voice and her own rapid, smooth rhythm as she rose to meet him, striving to overcome their separateness while he carried her to a place where there was no reality but him.

The earth and sky and woods seemed to explode with the force of their coming.

Afterward, they lay wrapped in each other's arms on the grass, Alex's body wrapped protectively around her, his face buried in her hair.

Floating between sleep and wakefulness, Kit watched the moon set.

TEN

Sheriff Eugene Mueller settled his huge bulk into a chair drawn up to Alex's kitchen table and accepted Consuelo's offer of iced tea. He wiped his sweaty forehead with the back of his khaki sleeve, licked his lips in anticipation, and downed the tea in great, gulping swallows. He set the glass down with a thud and nodded gratefully when Consuelo refilled it. "It's hotter than a coot out there," he said.

Kit almost laughed at Consuelo's puzzled look. For twenty years, since she'd first heard the sheriff use the expression, Kit hadn't been sure how hot a coot was, or even *what* it was.

"Sure is," Jake said knowingly, and Alex nodded agreement. Clearly, the temperature of coots was a secret known only to men. She caught Consuelo's gaze and smiled. The older woman rolled up her eyes.

The sheriff scratched one of the thin puffs of white hair growing from his freckled, sunburned scalp and frowned. The action narrowed his hazel eyes, making them seem tiny in his broad, sun-and-wind-roughened face. "I don't like to have to tell you this, folks," he said, giving Kit a cursory glance and then homing in on Alex, "but the fire marshal has just completed his investigation of the fire, and it looks like we got a case of arson here."

Shock rendered Kit speechless, but Consuelo raised her hand to her mouth. *"Madre de Dios!"*

Jake swore with the efficiency of long practice.

Alex sat very still, silver flashing in his eyes like lightning in storm clouds. "You're sure?"

"Oh, we're sure, all right. The marshal says it was strictly an amateur job. Looks like he—or they—took some rags from a pile your construction crew left, put them in the corner of one of the stalls, poured gas on them, and threw on a match. Would have been more efficient if they'd just poured the gas around, but they probably wanted to give themselves a lot of time to get off the property before anybody spotted the fire."

Kit inhaled in three shaky breaths. Who would want to burn the horses to death? A shudder wracked her. It had to be a stranger—a passerby bent on mischief, or one of the construction workers or deliverymen. No one who worked with horses would do anything so cruel . . . would they?

Alex's dangerously glittering gaze never left the sheriff's face. "Do you have any suspects?"

"Afraid not. We been over the place with a fine-toothed comb, but we haven't found a thing.'' He splayed a short-fingered hand over his formidable belly, and Kit knew he was longing for the bottle of Maalox he kept on the passenger side of his squad car. ''Trouble with arson is that most all the clues get burned.'' He took another gulp of iced tea. ''You got any enemies, Mr. Menendez?''

Alex's lips thinned. ''A few.''

The sheriff smiled, showing very large, very white teeth with a great gap between the middle two. ''I heard about you and Blane Wentworth. I'd have liked to have seen that.''

''You'd have had to arrest me.''

''I'd have wanted to give you a medal. If his daddy had tanned that Blane's hide when he should have . . .'' The sheriff waggled his broad head. ''Come to think of it, I can understand why he didn't. Blane's a chip off the old block.''

''I can't believe that Blane would do something as horrible as setting fire to a barn!'' Kit said.

Alex looked at her for a long moment, then he said, ''Why? Because he has a pedigree almost as long as yours?''

''Of course not!'' she snapped.

''He ordered his men to rough up you and the colt,'' Alex said in a flat, cold voice. ''He threatened me. He was furious when Copper King beat Nightwatch.''

''But he did and said all those things when he was angry. That's not the same as planning to set fire to the barn and sneaking in just before dawn and—''

"I agree with Kit," the sheriff said. "People'll do a lot of things when they're mad they wouldn't do if they took the time to think about them." The sheriff drained his glass of tea and heaved himself to his feet with a grunt. "But I can talk to Blane if you want me to."

"That won't be necessary." Alex's gaze drifted back to Kit, who watched him curiously. "I want proof before I accuse a prominent member of the community of doing anything improper."

"That's wise," the sheriff said. " 'Specially with you bein' new here and all. I'll just be on my way now. If you folks think of anything else, give me a call."

Alex saw the sheriff out and returned to the kitchen. "I knew when I bought this place that I might be unwelcome in the neighborhood, but arson comes as something of a surprise."

"It's bad enough to think it was arson, but I want to believe—I *have* to believe that it was a vicious, vicious prank by a stranger. That Blane or someone else we know did it is just unimaginable," Kit said.

Alex's big hands fisted. "Maybe in your world, but not in mine."

"What now, Alex?" Jake asked.

Consuelo's eyes were huge and dark and bewildered. "*Sí*, what?"

"I'll have a guard posted by Copper King's stall at the Lansing Farm."

"That beautiful colt. He is in danger?" Consuelo asked.

"Until we get to the bottom of this, we have to assume he is."

Kit caught her lower lip between her teeth and stared at him. Copper King's victory in the Commencement Stakes had made her think she was regaining control of her life.

But last night she'd made love to Alex—something she'd vowed she wouldn't do again. Today she discovered that someone had tried to kill the colt.

Everything was spinning out of control again.

She heaved a long, weary sigh, her shoulders slumping, her lips tightening with resignation. "What else can we do?"

"Go down to the barn and look for clues the sheriff might have overlooked," Alex said, and held out his hand. "Care to join me?"

Kit tried to wipe a smudge from Alex's cheek and grimaced with dismay when she made it worse. After an hour of picking through the burned-out barn, her hands were impossibly filthy.

"When you touch me, I want to touch you," Alex said, "but if I put my hands on you, everyone would see where they've been." He held up his sooty hands, then paused, a frown creasing his brow. "Still"—a small smile tugged at the corners of his lips—"there might be a way of getting around that."

He laid his arms across her shoulders, and with a nudge of his elbows brought her against him to nestle her body against his. She uttered a startled cry when she felt his hard, thrusting arousal against her belly.

"You see? I had something on my mind besides hunting for clues." He ran his lips over hers and when she moved her head forward to receive his kiss, he drew away a fraction and smiled teasingly down at her. "Ask me what I had on my mind, woman, or I swear I'll never kiss you again."

"What?" she asked instantly, her head flirtatiously cocked, her gaze on his lips.

"I was thinking that we could both use a bath. Together, this time."

Her breathing grew shallow and, embarrassed at her response, she drew back, then gasped when she felt his leg slide between hers. He brought his leg up slowly so that she was riding his muscled thigh. The flaming intimacy of the contact left her disoriented. She swallowed hard and her voice was tremulous when she said, "I—I thought we were looking for clues."

"There's no reason our search shouldn't be . . ."— he nibbled her earlobe—". . . stimulating."

She shouldn't have let down her guard and flirted with him, even for an instant, she thought. Then she stopped thinking and gave herself up to him, reveling in the hard, muscled strength of him, the softness of the lips that descended on hers. He'd become an addiction, an obsession, and, for a time at least, she was helpless in the grip of her desire.

At last they broke apart, breathless. "Someone . . . might come in," Alex said brokenly.

She took a deep, shuddering breath. "Yes," she

murmured, removing her shaking arms from around his neck. She pivoted away from him and forced her attention back to her surroundings. Blue sky and puffs of clouds showed through gaping holes in the roof and many of the roof beams lay across the barn's wide center aisle like giant, blackened Tinker toys. The heavy, acrid smell of smoke lingered in the air, while thick mud sucked at her boots and made her footing treacherous.

She peered into the darkness where Copper King's stall had been and shook her head. Their search was hopeless. They were not going to find a clue to connect Blane—or anyone else—to the fire.

But Alex wouldn't give up. He was on his hands and knees sifting through a pile of soggy ashes, his brow furrowed with concentration. Kit squatted and poked a tentative hand into a jumble of boards that lay near the spot where Sheriff Mueller said the fire had begun.

"Kit, come here!"

She moved to Alex's side and dropped to her knees. A black, cylindrical object lay across his grimy palm. She took it and held it up to the light slanting in from one of the holes in the roof.

It was a cigar stub.

Her stomach clenched and she felt nauseated, bile rising in her throat. She closed her eyes then opened them to look at Alex steadily. "It's not proof, you know."

"Not the kind of proof that would stand up in court, but it's all we've got," he said slowly, "and maybe we can use it to our advantage anyway." He stood, a hard look in his gray eyes. "I'm sure as hell going to find out."

Charles Lansing stopped his midnight-blue Rolls Royce in front of the Wentworth mansion and cut the engine. He smiled at Kit and Alex with more than usual sweetness, tilted his elegant silver head, and winked. "Don't worry, you two. This is going to work. While Hal Davis isn't any dumber than a rock, he isn't any smarter, either." He waved a slim-fingered hand toward the house. "So let's get started, shall we? We don't want to keep Blane and Hal waiting."

Charles's joke about Hal lightened the mood for a moment, and Kit was able to laugh, but as soon as they got out of the car, worry gnawed at her again. Alex's plan had seemed so clever when he'd proposed it to Charles. Now she wasn't so sure. If Blane and Hal didn't take the bait, Copper King might never be safe again no matter how many men Alex hired to guard him.

When Harrison ushered them into the library, Blane rose slowly from one of the two burgundy leather sofas facing each other across a huge mahogany coffee table, extended his hand to Charles, nodded to Kit, and glowered in Alex's direction. Hal Davis, standing in front of the fireplace, kept his beefy hands at his sides and nodded a greeting, his tiny eyes narrowed suspiciously. He rolled his cigar nervously between his teeth.

"Well," Blane said, after they were seated on the sofa facing him, "what's all this about?"

Charles took a plastic bag from the inside pocket of his jacket, opened it, extracted the cigar stub, and placed it on the coffee table. "This," he said simply.

Blane looked blank. "I don't understand."

Hal audibly exhaled, his black eyes darting from Charles to Blane. "Lotsa guys smoke cigars. Doesn't prove a thing."

Alex's voice was cold and hard as steel. "What makes you think we're trying to prove something, Davis?"

"Come, come, now," Blane said condescendingly. "We know your little delegation isn't here just to return a half-smoked cigar that may or may not belong to Hal. What do you think he's done?"

"I found the cigar in my burned-out barn, Wentworth," Alex almost shouted.

"As Hal rather inelegantly said, many men smoke cigars."

Alex opened his mouth to reply, but Charles laid a restraining hand on his forearm and said, "Alex assures me that his grooms aren't allowed to smoke in the barn, and that none of them smokes cigars."

"The center aisle of the barn is cleaned every evening, so the cigar must have been dropped there after the cleaning and before the fire broke out the next morning," Kit said.

"That was the first night Copper King was home after winning the race," Charles added.

Hal spat out a curse. "I ain't the only one who hates Menendez. Lotsa guys think people like him shouldn't be allowed here 'cept as stablehands—*if* they mind their manners."

Alex's fists clenched, but he said nothing. *Good, darling,* Kit thought. *Let Charles handle this. It's his job as president of the Thoroughbred Association, and you must see that all of us don't share Blane and Hal's prejudices.*

Charles steepled his slim fingers and looked serenely at Hal over them. "It's odd that you're the only person I've heard express that opinion."

Blane's lips curled back from his perfectly capped teeth. "I agree with Hal," he snapped, turning a look of sheer hatred on Alex. "Like most of his kind, Menendez lies. He planted this *evidence* to discredit Hal."

"Why would he do that?" Charles asked mildly.

"To get at me! He resents me because I'm everything he's not. I have birth, breeding, a place in society, the Wentworth name. Menendez was a common stablehand who worked for us until Hal fired him. Did he tell you that?"

Charles gave a little wave of dismissal. "Of course. I explained that his background doesn't matter—only the kind of man he is."

Blane's face swelled and grew with rage. "You're a traitor to your class."

"Perhaps," Charles said, smiling blandly, "but I think most of the people around here are united in their high opinion of Alex. When he says he thinks Hal might have set fire to his barn and offers us some proof, we at least consider the idea."

"You got no proof," Hal Davis repeated.

Charles looked at him coolly. "What if I said we had a witness?"

"You couldn't have! There was nobody—" A look of stunned horror settled on Hal Davis's face. "I mean—"

Kit's gaze flew from Hal to Alex. His face was still and composed. Only his steely gray eyes and his large hands clenching and unclenching in his lap betrayed his emotions. She knew he wanted those big, strong hands around Hal's neck, yet he held back.

Blane's flush turned nearly purple. He glanced around the circle of staring faces, then focused his angry gaze on Hal. "You're fired," he said in a tight, low voice.

"But I thought—"

"Fired!" Blane ground out the word through clenched teeth.

Hal jabbed a stubby forefinger at Alex. "But you told me you hated this bastard. You told me you wished his nag was dead! I did what I thought you wanted! I swear—"

"Get out, Hal. Get off Wentworth Farm. I don't want to see you again."

"But I've worked here for twenty-five years! I worked for your father . . ."

"Get out!"

Hal's face slackened and his massive shoulders slumped. He gave one strangled sob, turned, and lurched from the room.

Silence pulsed in the vast space, then Blane cleared his throat and said, "Hal was a long-time employee. In view of that, I'd like to keep this whole thing as quiet as possible. If you promise not to press charges against him, I'll pay for the damage to the barn."

"Oh, you'll do that in any event," Charles said, his aristocratic voice smooth as honey. "You'll build Alex a barn to replace the one that burned down that's just as fine as the one he's building for himself."

Blane swallowed and nodded slowly without looking at Alex. A bitter pill, Kit thought, and richly deserved.

"Alex will have to decide what else he wants from you now that he knows for certain Hal is guilty."

Astonishment flared in Blane's eyes. "But you knew he was guilty when you came in here. You have a witness."

Charles winked at Alex. "I merely asked what Hal would do if I *said* we had a witness. I didn't say there actually *was* one."

Blane's blue eyes went cold and flat. "You tricked him," he said dully.

"It was Alex's idea, actually. I think it worked out rather well."

"You bastards!" Blane said in a dry whiplash voice.

Alex's smile didn't reach his eyes. "When we came in here, we only had circumstantial evidence, but now there are witnesses to Hal's confession. What's more, we heard him say he set fire to my barn because you wanted Copper King dead." Alex sat back comfortably. "It should be an interesting trial."

"No!" Blane's voice was high and thin with fear.

"I've offered to set it right! What more can I do? I have a reputation . . . my parents in Palm Beach . . . What will they say? What will their friends think?" His voice broke, then he raised his head and squared his shoulders. "Hal lied. I never said I wanted the horse dead."

"I believe you did," Charles said. "What's more, when the story of what happened here this afternoon comes out, most of your neighbors will, too. They all know Hal never had an original thought in his life." His gaze narrowed on Blane's face. "And they know what kind of a man you are."

Blane's face was somehow fuller than Kit had ever seen it, as if someone had inflated it with helium. His eyes were blue ice, angry and scared. "All this will come out," he said brokenly, mouthing the words as if he didn't quite comprehend them.

Alex and Charles exchanged a look, a silent communication passing between them. "Not . . . necessarily," Charles said slowly.

Hope flared in Blane's eyes. "How much do you want? I can raise—"

"I expect you to replace what your man destroyed, Wentworth, but you can't buy your way out of this completely," Alex snapped.

"Then what do you want from me?" A note of hysteria crept into Blane's voice.

"I want you out of here," Alex said in a voice that trembled with the anger he was fighting to hold in check. "And I want you out of racing. Sell your share in Wentworth Farm and the horses and get out."

Stunned, Blane simply gaped at him.

"You run your horses too often, Blane," Charles said, the first hint of anger creeping into his soft, cultivated voice, "and you train them too harshly. You've ruined more good horses than you've ever brought to the track," Charles said. "You and your father before you shame everyone who owns and loves thoroughbred horses. You always have."

"Hal—"

"Was cruel," Kit cut in, "but he was only the trainer. You set the standards for your employees. You're responsible."

Blane stared at them in mute fury, and Kit's mouth went dry as cotton. *Please,* she thought. *Please let him agree to this.* For what seemed an eternity she studied him for the first sign of uncertainty, then saw his hard, handsome face go slack.

He spoke on a sigh. "All . . . right."

She couldn't resist a glance at Alex. She caught the swift gleam of triumph in his eyes, the slight relaxation of his muscles. "I want you to write what we dictate, then sign it," Alex said.

"My word isn't good enough, I suppose." After a few moments of silence that spoke volumes, Blane stood, walked to a desk near the window, took out pen and paper, and returned to his seat on the sofa. The pen poised above the paper, he glowered at Alex.

"Write that you heard Hal Davis admit to burning my barn, and that he did it because he heard you say that you hated me and wanted my colt, Copper King, dead."

Biting his lower lip, his hand shaking with anger, Blane wrote.

"Now date and sign your statement."

Blane did as he was ordered.

"Give it to us so we can witness it." When the three of them had signed, Alex folded the paper and put it into his breast pocket. "I warn you, Wentworth. If you don't live up to your agreement, or if anything happens to my horses or property in the future, I'll make this public."

Charles nodded. "And if Alex doesn't, I will. You are to sell this place and your horses as soon as possible and slip away quietly or subject yourself to public disgrace when we prosecute Hal Davis, as we will if you don't adhere to the letter of our agreement." For the first time, Charles permitted himself to smile at Blane. "I think the first choice is the better one, don't you?"

Blane sneered at him. "You've sold out your own people, Lansing. You're siding with a stablehand and a—"

"I owe this former stablehand a great deal for his decision not to prosecute Hal. I love this community, and a trial might have torn it apart." Charles's gaze moved to Kit and Alex. "Shall we go? I think we've accomplished what we came for."

They'd begun to walk toward the door when Blane's voice, hard with hate, stopped them. "Wait until my father hears that Charles Lansing, pillar of the community, president of the Thoroughbred Breeders' Association, has taken the side of a Mexican stablehand and a gambler's daughter against a Wentworth!''

A voice inside Kit gave a long, soundless howl of grief and fury. Her breathing stopped, her movements stilled. She ran Blane's words through her mind again. *A gambler's daughter.* How had he known?

She saw Alex through the swift, sudden sheen of her tears. It seemed that some powerful, tidal grief was pulling at him, sucking his breath, washing the color from his face.

Oh, my darling, the voice inside her cried. *I didn't want you to know!*

She stumbled toward the door, and over the rush of blood in her ears she heard Blane's voice again. ''. . . gambled away the fortune and Randall Farm. Everybody thinks Oliver was a saint, but he wasn't. He was nothing but a—''

Charles slammed the library door behind them.

The ride back to Randall Farm was silent—Alex a dark, brooding presence in the backseat. As soon as the luxurious car purred to a stop, he thanked Charles, got out, and hurried into the house.

She read rage and grief in his jerky movements and in the slump of his massive shoulders, and she wanted to run after him and say . . . what? She turned her bewildered, stricken gaze to Charles.

His blue eyes were filled with worry and pain. ''I knew about Oliver's debts and how he incurred them, Kit. I tried to help him, as he'd helped me years ago when a business deal of mine went sour, but he refused my help and he refused to get therapy for his addiction.'' Charles shook his head sadly. "The Randall pride. It was Oliver's greatest virtue and his greatest weakness."

"How did Blane learn about . . . about . . ." Her voice faded, trailed away.

"Who knows how a vicious gossip like Wentworth learns anything? Perhaps he saw Oliver one day at the track. There was a kind of . . . frenzy about him when he was gambling. For someone familiar with the symptoms, it must have been unmistakable." Charles took Kit's hand. "I know how much your father meant to Alex. Finding out about Oliver—especially that way—must have hurt a lot, but Alex will get over it. Just give him time."

Tears sheened in her eyes. "I wish I could be as sure of that as you are." She refused Charles's offer to drive her to Jake's and got out of the car. She needed to walk. She set off across the lawn, then paused as a light came on in Alex's room and his silhouette appeared behind the curtains on the French doors. He began to pace rapidly across the vast width of the room, raking his fingers through his hair.

She had to go to him, to try to explain. She threw back her shoulders determinedly, walked to the doors, and knocked before she had a chance to reconsider. When he jerked open the door, she stepped back, wanting to run, but his intense gaze impaled her. She paused, motionless and scared.

"Well?" he demanded.

"I . . . I have to talk to you."

He nodded and stepped aside. "Come in."

Except for Alex's bed, a packing crate-turned-nightstand and a lamp, the room was as empty as the eyes he turned on her. "Tell me what Wentworth said was a lie, Kit."

She forced herself to look at him without blinking. "I can't." Her body sagged. She buried her hands in the pockets of her skirt and chewed her lower lip worriedly, uncertain how to continue. "It *is* true . . . but there were reasons for what my father did. He wasn't . . . well . . . toward the end. He—"

Alex cut off her words with a slicing hand. "He pretended to be something he wasn't. He fooled people. He fooled *me* into thinking he was the kind of man I wanted to be." Alex pushed his tumbled hair back from his forehead, his brow furrowed with pain and bewilderment. "All my adult life, I wanted to live the kind of life he lived." Alex's voice broke. "But he was a phony and a failure. His life was a lie."

"No!" Her voice was ragged in her throat. "That's not—"

"And you—you lied to me, too, Kit," he said, the grief thick and heavy in his voice. "And now"— he looked around the nearly empty room—"I don't know what to do with this place, with—" He stopped, and his eyes, fixed on the middle distance, slowly grew blank again.

With my life. He didn't need to finish the sentence. Kit heard the words as clearly as if he'd spoken them. She stood very still, her heart beating so loudly she imagined he must hear it.

"I'm leaving for a while, Kit."

No, she cried silently. She read the terrible hurt in

his eyes and drew in a deep, ragged breath, then nodded. "I understand."

He smiled the tiniest, most fleeting of smiles. "When I vowed to solve the mystery of Kit Randall, I never imagined anything like this," he said, and turned away from her to look out the window at the black, moonless sky.

ELEVEN

When Consuelo called, Alex had just finished packing the last of the items from his Summit Enterprises office and was about to turn over his key to the new president's secretary. His mood had gotten blacker each day of the two weeks he'd been in San Francisco completing the sale of his company, and his tone was sharp when he said, "Hello."

"Kit has gone," his aunt said without preliminary.

His gut tightened and his hand clenched hard around the receiver. "Gone? Gone *where?*"

"I do not know. This morning she packed her car and said goodbye to Jake and me and drove away. She said she would write to us when she gets to her new home, but that she does not know yet where it will be."

"But she has a contract," he found himself protesting.

"She almost broke it before," Consuelo said. "Why should you be surprised that she at last did it?" The line was silent for a moment. Then: "You have treated her badly, Alejandro. Do you not think it hurts her, too, that her father gambled away her birthright—the farm, those beautiful horses—all the things she loved best?"

The anguish that he'd been trying hard to hold at bay slid into his mind and settled there. His throat tightened. Consuelo was right. Oliver had hurt him, but he'd hurt Kit more.

"Kit is a good person, and I have always thought her father was a great man. I still do, especially when I think of all he did for you and for so many others. No one is perfect, and if you think they are and you seek to imitate them, you set a standard for yourself that you will never meet. You will always be unhappy." Consuelo paused a moment, then said, "As unhappy as you were before you fell in love with Kit."

"I'm not—" One of the smoke-glass mirrors on the opposite wall of the office reflected his face, and he saw the shock there, unfeigned and profound. Then another emotion surged over him, warming his skin, his blood, the very marrow of his bones. He felt his breath go out of him in a rush. He *was* in love with Kit!

And he knew just when it happened. She'd been on her knees, inching forward in the burning barn, pulling the colt behind her. Her tiny, rasping voice had come from near the floor asking for his help, and he'd felt a need to protect her unlike anything he'd ever experienced before. He should have recognized the symptoms then instead of talking himself into believing that all he wanted was an affair.

He cursed silently. He'd been a damned fool. He'd get her back, and . . .

For the briefest of instants, he felt giddy with a sudden lightness. Then reality dropped its heavy weight upon him and his body slumped. Kit was gone, and even if she came back or he found her, things wouldn't be the same between them. He'd rejected her and denounced her father. She couldn't forget that, or forgive it. But futile as it might be, he had to find her, to talk with her. "Jake has no idea where she is?" His voice rasped in his throat.

"No, and he is almost frantic with worry. I am scared for him."

"Tell him to try to relax. I'll find her. I promise." After he'd hung up, he drummed his fingers on the desk, frowning, silently cursing himself for thinking only of his own pain and anger. Kit had nothing to to with what her father had done. She hadn't lied, she only hadn't told him.

And he, Alex Menendez, had behaved like a first-class jerk. The thought infuriated him and he surged out of his chair, jammed his hands into his pockets, and began to pace the large room. He finally stopped in front of the huge plate-glass window to stare out at the breathtaking sweep of San Francisco without seeing it. "Think, Menendez," he muttered, "who'd know where she is?"

He began to pace again, then jerked to a halt and brought his fist down on the desk with enough force to rattle the desk lamp and sent a couple of pens skittering across the polished surface. "That's it!" he growled. "She'll know if anyone does."

He strode across the room and rummaged through several boxes until he found his Rolodex. He riffled through it with shaking fingers, stalked back to the telephone, and punched in the Lansings' number.

Kit arrived at the Pacific Inn in Big Sur on a day so blue and gold and windswept that being alive in it was like being half drunk. She'd made a wise choice, she told herself. She'd bask in all this beauty and let it drift into her and take away the pain of Alex's rejection.

Arthur Marlowe, the owner of the inn, who managed to look like an English don in spite of his wildly incongruous sandals, cut-off jeans, and too-large Budweiser T-shirt, struggled ahead of her up the steep trail toward the cottage she'd rented. He drooped under the weight of her largest suitcases, made heavy by a dozen of her father's diaries. Now and then Arthur smiled a brilliant, white-toothed smile at her over his shoulder.

"Just a little farther," he said breathlessly.

They lurched out of the forest and into a large, sunlit clearing, and there was the cottage, long and low and rambling. Kit gave a little gasp of pure pleasure. "It looks enchanted!"

The tiny house was made of random boards that had weathered in the sun and wind to a silvery gray. Its wood-shingled roof had caught the rain and sea breezes and formed a bright green shaggy moss like the green of the surrounding meadow. Across the front was a wide, deep-roofed porch, and Kit knew before she walked the rest of the way to stand there that over the treetops she'd see the Pacific stretching into the distance beneath the blue-gold sky.

She filled her lungs with the light, pure air, then exhaled it. "Ohhh . . . it's wonderful. I remember your inn from my childhood, but there were so many little cabins tucked away on these winding paths. I never saw them all. This must be be one of the loveliest."

Arthur dropped the suitcases in front of the door, raked the thatch of white hair from his eyes with a nut-brown hand, and followed her gaze. "I think it's the most beautiful one we have, although other people have their favorites." He glanced sideways at her. "This cabin—this whole place—is good for what ails you."

She looked at him levelly. "I'm sure it is."

He unlocked the door, handed her the key, and they entered a low-ceilinged room beamed with rough pine logs. A huge, freestanding stone fireplace with a comfortable-looking old sofa sitting before it dominated the room. On the coffee table in front of the sofa a bottle of champagne chilled in a silver ice bucket. A fire crackled cheerfully in the fireplace.

Arthur led her around the fireplace to the sleeping area, where an enormous bed took up most of the space. It was very old and very fine—a four-poster shrouded in a canopy of lacy, creamy fabric and piled high with a light, airy comforter and many frothy pillows of all shapes and sizes.

A bridal bed.

He set down her suitcases. "This is the closest thing we have to a bridal suite. It was our only vacant cottage." He lifted his slim shoulders apologetically. "We have a couple checking out tomorrow. Maybe you'd like their place, but you'll have to stay here tonight."

She lifted a restraining hand. "This is fine . . . really."

"I'll leave you then." He headed for the door. "Call us if there's anything you need, Ms. Randall. We serve dinner at seven."

An hour later she'd unpacked, bathed, slipped on a terry-cloth robe, and taken a flute of champagne out to the porch. She looked out to sea, where the afternoon was fading to a last glow of unearthly beauty.

She twirled the icy cold, long-stemmed glass between her fingers and took a long swallow of champagne. It slid smoothly down her throat, ice turning to fire when it reached her stomach. She closed her eyes. She'd waited for Alex for two weeks and he hadn't come back. She'd continued to train Copper King, seen the new barn completed and the horses moved in and the burned-out barn razed. She'd supervised the regrading and paving of the roads, the relandscaping of the lake, the plowing and replanting of the paddocks. Each afternoon she'd faxed a memo to Alex telling of the day's progress.

She had received no answer.

He'd lost interest in the farm. He was allowing work to continue only so that he could command top dollar when he resold it. She drew in a long, ragged breath. "My poor darling," she whispered into the deepening twilight, "what do you build your life on now?" Tears rose behind her eyelids.

A full moon hung over the treetops and a breeze rose. She shivered and drew her robe more tightly around her, drained the last of the champagne, and went into the cottage.

The Big Sur Inn prided itself on providing no television for its guests, and she found herself with little to distract her. She wandered aimlessly around the cabin for a while, stirred the fire, and at last sank down onto the comfortable old sofa with several of her father's diaries in her hands. There were forty-three diaries altogether—one for each year since Oliver had received his first leather-bound, gold-stamped volume on his twelfth birthday. She'd packed the most recent ones and left the others in the trunk of her car.

Her father had been a meticulous record-keeper, and she'd always meant to read them for the historical record he provided of the day-to-day life of Randall Farm, and for his insights into breeding and training methods.

She ran a forefinger over a diary. Now she wanted to read them for another purpose—to reach out to him, to know that there was someone else who'd shared her love of Randall Farm and her horror and sadness at its loss. And she wanted someone to assuage the loneliness, to pierce the silence that stretched around her.

But she couldn't quite bring herself to read the

latest diaries—not yet. Instead, she selected a diary that described the time before her mother's death, when Kit had been a college freshman in Paris. She felt a quick tightening in her throat when she read of how much her father had missed her, but overall the diary reflected a happy, successful man, proud of his life and his place in the community—a man who still adored his wife after twenty years of marriage.

A man who depended on his wife too much. Kit's mother had made every financial decision, balanced the farm's books, and run the place with a shrewd business sense her husband lacked. Kit smiled wryly. Olivia Clemens Randall had not been born to vast wealth as her husband had, and she'd had a healthy respect for a dollar.

With mounting tension, Kit selected another diary— this one for the year of her mother's death. Kit passed over the account of the death—even now it would be too painful—and concentrated on its aftermath. Oliver had been cut loose in a world he couldn't cope with. He actually considered it bad form to negotiate with his suppliers for the best prices—or even to *ask* the prices—and anyone who'd claimed to be from a charity, no matter how poorly credentialed, could be sure of a huge contribution.

Then the gambling had begun.

At first he'd bet small amounts on occasional races, and only when he was at the track to see his own horses run. Later, he'd gone to the track just to bet, and the amounts had become larger, the bets more frequent. Soon it was clear he was in the grip of a compulsion.

For a while, Kit stopped reading, unable to decipher the writing through the blur of her tears. Her father hadn't understood the implications of what he was doing then. To a Randall, having money was as natural as having air to breathe. Oliver could not imagine a time when he'd have no more.

Kit walked around the cabin, his arms folded across her chest, her breath catching in her throat. She steeled herself for what was to come. Then she stirred the fire, sank down on the sofa, and picked up the last diary with a hand that shook almost violently.

Her father's writing had changed. It was increasingly agitated, then almost indecipherable as the implications of what he'd done finally became clear to him. The final entry told of a trip to see his banker in San Francisco, of agonized, desperate calls to other creditors.

And then these words:

I could ask Alex Menendez for help. As wealthy as many of my friends are, he's the only man I know with the resources to cover my debts and the discretion to say nothing about them. If I'd had a son, I'd have liked him to be like Alex—strong and generous and kind behind his tough exterior. It's strange that after all these years, and all the friends I've made, a man I've seen fewer than a dozen times in the past twenty years is the one I think of now.

But I can't ask Alex for anything. I want him

to think of me as I was when he was young—
as confident and determined as he is now.

Her fingers suddenly limp, Kit dropped the diary
back onto the coffee table, huddled down into the
embracing softness of the sofa, drew up her knees,
and began to cry. She wept until she was out of
tears and then went to bed and slept an exhausted,
dreamless sleep.

Sometime just before dawn she drifted out of sleep
and thought, *Near the end, he was thinking of you,
my darling. I wonder what you'd say if you knew
that?* Then she let the gray sucking tide of exhaustion
pull her back under.

She awoke to loud, persistent knocking on the
door. She groaned and threw her feet over the side
of the bed, blinking into the light. From the angle
of the sun on the window she judged it was well past
noon. Wrapping her robe around her, she padded
barefoot into the living room. "Who is it?"

"Alex."

She paused on a swift intake of breath and pulled
her hand back from the doorknob.

"Let me in."

She stared at the door uncertainly. For so long
she'd wanted him to come to her, and now, when
he had, she felt a swift rush of fear that was near
panic. What did he want? What could she say to
him?

"This is a pretty cabin. I'd hate to break the door

down, but that's exactly what I'll do if you don't open it right now."

Her breath left her lungs in a rush. She knew he'd do it. Pursing her lips to stop their trembling, she opened the door and stood aside. "How did you—?"

He strode past her. "Caroline Lansing has a long memory. She said you and your family had vacationed here, and that you always loved the place. When I asked for you at the desk the guy in the Budweiser T-shirt seemed only too eager to tell me what cabin you were in." He smiled humorlessly. "Why did you run away, Kit?"

Alex looked exhausted. The grooves on either side of his mouth were deeper, the lines that fanned from the corners of his eyes more pronounced. The eyes were rimmed by black smudges and bloodshot under his long, thick lashes. His unruly hair tumbled onto his forehead, and his strong, square chin and jaw were peppered with stubble.

He jammed his hands into the pockets of his wrinkled gray slacks and hunched his shoulders belligerently, anger crackling around him like an electric current. "Have you forgotten we have a contract?" His voice was low, tight with fury.

Kit belted her robe more securely around her, lifted her chin, and met his gaze squarely. "No, I haven't forgotten." Her palms turned wet and her breath came in short, gasping chunks.

"Then why did you leave?"

She just looked at him, trying to breathe from her diaphragm to still the churning in her stomach.

When it was clear she wasn't going to answer, he said, "I want you to come back to the farm."

They locked gazes for an angry instant. "I have no intention of doing that," she said, her voice rising.

"If you don't, I'll—"

"*What*? Sue me?"

"That's exactly what I'll do," he said in a voice thick with menace.

"Go ahead! I haven't got a dime."

He paled, and the fury seemed to drain from him. "*What*?"

She gave a short, angry laugh. "I think you heard me."

"I heard you, all right, but I find what you said hard to believe. I paid top dollar for the farm . . . millions."

"My father *owed* millions. His life insurance enabled me to stay afloat as long as I did"—she raked her hand through the thick tangle of her hair—"but I spent every spare minute juggling the money to cover the bills from the suppliers, to make the payroll . . ." She gave a small sigh of resignation and defeat. "There's just enough to get me through the next few weeks while I look for a job. "This"—she threw out her hand in a gesture that encompassed the cabin—"is a luxury I really can't afford. I just . . . wanted to say goodbye to the place I loved so much as a child." She felt tears rise behind her eyes, and turning away from him, squeezed them shut.

"You have nothing left." It wasn't a question, just a speaking out loud of something he seemed to find hard to grasp any other way.

"And now that you know there's nothing to be gained by suing me, why don't you leave? I don't think we have anything more to say to each other." She cast a look at him over her shoulder.

He waved away her words. "On the contrary. We have a lot to say to each other, and I'm not leaving here until we say it. Why did you run, Kit?" he persisted, taking a step toward her, dropping his hands to her shoulders, and turning her to face him.

"I don't want to talk about this. I just want to put it all behind me. Please, please leave." She found herself shaking so badly she could barely stand.

He released her, but he continued to study her grimly. "Not a chance."

She was silent for a moment. "All right," she said, and gave a long, ragged sigh. "I knew how you felt about my father . . . how you felt about me. I thought you wouldn't want to see me anymore, that I'd just be a reminder of the man who'd let you down, particularly because . . . because I'd pretended that he—and I—were something we weren't. I—I was . . . ashamed." She stared up at Alex, her eyes wide and moist with unshed tears, her lower lip trembling.

She wanted to go to him, to step into the hard circle of his arms, to lay her head against his chest, and to tell him that whatever he wanted, she'd give him just to be near him, just to see him occasionally.

She drew herself up stiffly and stayed where she was.

Alex rubbed his forehead wearily. "What are you

going to do now? How are you going to earn a living?"

This time the silence was longer. "I'll do the same thing I've always done. It's what I know. I—"

He put up a hand, a barrier to stop her voice. "Then come back and work at Randall Farm."

"And when you sell the farm? What do I do then?"

Surprise slackened his face. "What gave you the idea I was going to sell it?"

"When—when you didn't acknowledge my memos, I thought you'd lost interest, that—"

"I'll admit I was disillusioned and confused. I was furious with both you and your father, but after the initial shock of hearing the truth—and from a bastard like Wentworth"—Alex's lips tightened grimly—"I never, *never* wavered in my love of the farm or in my desire to keep it, and to pass it on to my children." He smiled wryly. "I want to see Copper King run the first Saturday in May—and to know that I own him."

Alex gripped her hand, led her to the sofa, and drew her down beside him. "I admit that for a while I felt empty and angry that the man who'd meant the most in my life hadn't been all I thought he was. I went back to complete the sale of Summit Enterprises"—a near-smile played on his lips and his eyes were silvery in the bright slant of sunlight from the window—"and to brood."

"Yesterday my aunt called and told me you'd left and she didn't know where you'd gone. I was mad at you for refusing to tell me about your father, but Consuelo set me straight as she always has.''

Frowning, he studied Kit's face. ''Can you forgive me for the way I treated you and for what I said about your father?''

She nodded. ''Of course. For a while I was pretty angry with him myself, and you had a right to resent it when I withheld the truth.'' She couldn't force her gaze to his. She looked straight ahead at the long-dead fire.

From the corner of her eye she saw Alex smile gently. ''I loved your father, Kit. Someone like you, coming from a happy, stable family, might not be able to understand what he meant to me, how important a father figure can be when you don't have a father. Sometimes I didn't see him for years, but I knew I could call him and he'd be there for me. Knowing that gave me the strength to accomplish what I have. As I told you, I wouldn't have been successful without him—without his example.'' He smiled ruefully. ''Or what I thought was his example.''

''He was everything you thought he was before my mother died—in the days when you knew him best, before his . . . illness consumed him.''

''I'm glad to know that.''

Unable to speak, Kit merely nodded, then picked up her father's last diary. After a few moments she turned to the last page and said, ''I think you should read this.'' She extended the diary to Alex.

As he read, his expression changed from surprise to a warm, gentle, loving look that almost took her breath away to a look of deep sadness. Shaking his head, Alex put down the diary. "If only he'd asked for help when he wanted to. If only he hadn't let his pride stand in the way."

Wordlessly she nodded.

Alex inhaled a great lungful of breath. "I guess I love him more than ever now."

Her gaze flew to Alex's and she raised her eyebrows in question.

"He was flawed, Kit. Human like the rest of us, not a superman. That makes him more understandable, someone a guy like me can emulate—not a paragon I have to worship."

She heard the echo of her own thoughts in Alex's words and she felt an explosion of love so great she thought her heart would burst with it. Love for her father, and more than anyone or anything, for Alex. She sat very still, her hands in her lap, and waited for the thrumming of her heart to slow.

"Whatever you did, it was for him, and I can't hold it against you. If our situations were reversed, I'd probably have done the same. Come back to Randall Farm with me. You belong there. You lost it through no fault of yours." She thought Alex's voice was admirably calm—particularly when her heart was thudding in her throat.

She clasped her hands tighter—so tight that little pinpricks of pain shot up her hands and wrists. "You have time to devote to the farm now that you've sold Summit Enterprises. You'll have Jake's advice on training Copper King. You don't need me, and I won't accept your charity."

"I'm not offering charity. I want you there. You belong at Randall Farm with Jake and Consuelo and Copper King—and with *me*."

"No!" she almost shouted. "I've said goodbye to everyone. I've made the break. I don't want the pain of waiting a few months and doing it all over again."

"You misunderstand me. I want you to stay permanently." His beautiful voice dropped very low. "You don't have to leave. Ever."

She sucked in a long, shuddering breath, then inhaled it. "What are you going to do? Appoint me Randall Farm's trainer-for-life?" *Or your mistress. I will not be your mistress!*

The ghost of a smile lifted the corners of his mouth. "How about becoming Mrs. Alejandro Menendez?"

There was a silence, dead and tangible in the room as she tried to catch her breath. She raised her chin a stubborn fraction of an inch. All she had to do was to keep her wits about her and remain calm. She wouldn't—she couldn't—lose her head this time. He'd said nothing about love, nothing of commitment. Summoning every ounce of her willpower, she managed to force out the words, "I can't."

Alex's gray eyes hardened, and his hand shot out and fisted in the thickness of her hair. "You still can't forget that you're a Randall, can you, Kit? You're a golden-haired princess from an old and aristocratic family. However much you want me—and I *know* you do—it comes back to that, doesn't it? I'm just not good enough!" He shouted the last words and she would have recoiled except that he held her too tightly.

Kit felt her breasts rise and fall with the sudden, searing heat of her emotion. "That's not true!"

"It *is* true! I tried to buy my way into an identity—into an entire way of life. I wanted to come as close as I could to being what Oliver was, maybe to what his son would have been if he'd had one"—Alex clenched his teeth and hard ridges appeared along his jaw and bulged in his powerful neck—"but I can't buy what you have and I was a fool to try. I'd have to be born to it." He let her go so suddenly that she almost fell.

He took a pen from his pocket, picked up her father's diary, and tore a blank page from it. He crouched beside the coffee table and, using it as a desk, he began to write—great, bold, slashing strokes that filled the page. Then he stood, shoved the paper toward her, and said, "Here. It will always be yours anyway."

His footsteps thudded on the pine floor as he strode to the door and jerked it open.

Kit didn't turn when the door slammed behind him. For long moments she stared at the paper while the writing swam into focus through the mist of tears.

She read with slowly dawning comprehension. Alex had given her back Randall Farm and the horses, along with a sum of money to complete the renovation that took her breath away! He'd sacrificed his dream for her. She had everything she'd wanted all her life here in her hand.

But now it wasn't enough.

Clutching the paper, she ran out of the cottage and across the clearing, oblivious to the sharp stones that tore at her feet. She caught up with Alex on the narrow trail leading down to the parking lot and, breathless, unable to speak, grabbed his arm.

He turned to look at her and his eyes were flat and dead. "I don't expect you to thank me."

"I didn't . . . come . . . to thank you," she managed to force out. "I followed you to say I can't accept this."

"Pride destroyed your father. Don't let it ruin you, too."

She tore the paper into tiny pieces that were caught by a breeze and scattered like dry leaves. Tears made cold, wet tracks down her cheeks, and suddenly, humiliatingly, she began to sob—great wracking sobs that shook her body and made her face and throat ache with their force.

Alex stood before her, his expression softening from fury to wonder. Then he brushed her tears away. "Don't cry, Kit," he pleaded. "Don't cry, my darling." Then he was lifting her, carrying her easily up the narrow trail toward the cottage.

He put her on the sofa and knelt before her. She felt fragile, almost brittle, as if she would crack into a million pieces at any moment. He'd given her back Randall Farm, he'd called her *darling*, he'd carried her here gently, almost reverently, whispering loving words in English and Spanish as he'd easily navigated the steep trail. Now he was looking up at her with a soft, almost luminous light in his gray eyes that she'd never seen there before, had never hoped to see.

He slid his arms around her waist. "Do you love me, Kit? Is that what your tears mean?"

She hesitated. He's said nothing of love, and he was asking her if *she* loved *him*, asking her to speak first, to compromise her pride.

Give it up, Kit. A voice screamed inside her head. *What's it brought you but misery? Risk yourself— just this once.* Catching her lower lip between her teeth, unable to meet Alex's eyes, she nodded. "I'll marry you on whatever terms you'll have me, not because of the farm, but because I love you," she said, staring first at her bare feet and then, gathering her courage, stealing a look at him.

Then he was beside her on the sofa. He pulled her into his arms, cupped her face in his hands, and looked at her with such love that she almost stopped breathing. "I love you, too, my darling—more than I can ever tell you, more than I can ever show you."

He kissed her—a long, passionate kiss that ended only when they were both out of breath and aching with longing. "Am I mistaken," he said, "or are you wearing absolutely nothing under that robe?"

A laugh rose in her throat. She slanted a teasing look at him, put her lips very close to his ear, and whispered in a low, sexy voice, "Absolutely . . . *nothing.*"

He made a low sound, somewhere between a growl and a purr, and said, "And did I see a very inviting four-poster in your bedroom?"

"*Our* bedroom," she corrected. "And it's very sexy. A bridal bed."

He lifted her again and moved toward the bedroom. "Let's sample it now and come back after we're married."

Kit wrapped her arms around his neck and rested her cheek against his chest. "I'd like to be married at Randall Farm, under the oak tree where I first saw you."

He grinned wickedly at her. "And where we made love. How could you forget that?"

She brushed his unruly hair from his forehead and shook her head, a smile on her lips. "I haven't. Not for a minute."

He laid her on the bed and she felt something warm and enormous and slow begin in her groin and spread outward, making her body languid, her movements slow. He stripped off his clothes, then her robe, and he lay beside her and drew her into his arms again . . .

And, in the twenty-eighth year of her life, Kit felt, at last, complete.

It was dark before they stopped making love, and when they rose from bed to dress for dinner, Alex stooped to pick up a picture that had fallen to the floor from the nightstand. It was of Copper King, draped with a blanket of flowers, in the winner's circle after the Commencement Stakes. Alex held it up. "No matter how many other horses we own, I'll always love him best because he brought us together."

Kit nodded, smiling, then frowned and chewed her lower lip thoughtfully. "I still think he has a good chance to win on the first Saturday in May if he stays healthy.''

Alex looked at her, his heart in his eyes. ''Even if he wins the Kentucky Derby, we'll have won something even better. The victory of our love is the sweetest victory of all.''

She cupped the lean, hard plane of his cheek in her palm and looked up at him, her throat choked with emotion. He was so tough, so masculine, and yet the look in his eyes was loving and gentle. ''Yes, my darling,'' she said. ''I know.''